PUFFIN BOOKS

STORIES FOR TENS AND OVER

This is a wide-ranging collection of stories which children between the ages of ten and thirteen are sure to enjoy. There is plenty of humour, varying from the bland innocence of P. G. Wodehouse's 'The Mixer' to the tortured delight in H. G. Wells's story, 'The Truth About Pyecraft'.

There are medieval and classical legends, two poignant modern stories by Philippa Pearce and Bill Naughton, a little-known but blood-curdling thriller, 'The Man and the Snake', and a delightful episode from Rudyard Kipling's *The Jungle Book*.

Stories for Tens and Over

EDITED BY
SARA AND STEPHEN CORRIN

Illustrated by Victor Ambrus

Puffin Books
in association with Faber and Faber

Puffin Books, Penguin Books Ltd, Harmondsworth, Middlesex, England
Penguin Books, 625 Madison Avenue, New York, New York 10022, U.S.A.
Penguin Books Australia Ltd, Ringwood, Victoria, Australia
Penguin Books Canada Ltd, 2801 John Street, Markham, Ontario, Canada L3R 1B4
Penguin Books (N.Z.) Ltd, 182–190 Wairau Road, Auckland 10, New Zealand

This collection first published (with four additional stories)
by Faber and Faber Limited 1976
Published in Puffin Books 1982
Reprinted 1982, 1983

Made and printed in Great Britain by
Richard Clay (The Chaucer Press) Ltd, Bungay, Suffolk
Set in Monophoto Baskerville

Contents

Contents

To the Reader

In this selection it is the story that matters above all else. Each one has cried out to be included. Most, though by no means all, fall readily into categories – classic or romantic epic, weirdie thriller, 'man and beast', humorous – but each is excellent of its kind. In addition to those based on myth and legend, there are powerful stories from some of our finest modern – and not so modern – authors and liveliest humorists. They range widely – France, the U.S., Italy, Greece; they delve into the remote past and glimpse into the sci-fi future.

Take your choice and good reading!

P . G . WODEHOUSE

The Mixer

He Meets a Shy Gentleman

Looking back, I always consider that my career as a dog proper really started when I was bought for the sum of half a crown by the Shy Man. That event marked the end of my puppyhood. The knowledge that I was worth actual cash to somebody filled me with a sense of new responsibilities. It sobered me. Besides, it was only after that half-crown changed hands that I went out into the great world; and, however interesting life may be in an East End public-house, it is only when you go out into the world that you really broaden your mind and begin to see things.

Within its limitations, my life had been singularly full and vivid. I was born, as I say, in a public-house in the East End, and however lacking a public-house may be in refinement and the true culture, it certainly provides plenty of excitement. Before I was six weeks old, I had upset three policemen by getting between their legs when they came round to the side-door, thinking they had heard suspicious noises; and I can still recall the interesting sensation of being chased seventeen times round the yard with a broom-handle after a well-planned and completely successful raid on

9

the larder. These and other happenings of a like nature soothed for the moment but could not cure the restlessness which has always been so marked a trait in my character. I have always been restless, unable to settle down in one place and anxious to get on to the next thing. This may be due to a gipsy strain in my ancestry – one of my uncles travelled with a circus – or it may be the Artistic Temperament, acquired from a grandfather who, before dying of a surfeit of paste in the property-room of the Bristol Coliseum, which he was visiting in the course of a professional tour, had an established reputation on the music-hall as one of Professor Pond's Performing Poodles.

I owe the fullness and variety of my life to this restlessness of mine, for I have repeatedly left comfortable homes in order to follow some perfect stranger who looked as if he were on his way to somewhere interesting. Sometimes I think I must have cat blood in me.

The Shy Man came into our yard one afternoon in April, while I was sleeping with mother in the sun on an old sweater which we had borrowed from Fred, one of the barmen. I heard mother growl, but I didn't take any notice. Mother is what they call a good watch-dog, and she growls at everybody except master. At first, when she used to do it, I would get up and bark my head off, but not now. Life's too short to bark at everybody who comes into our yard. It is behind the public-house, and they keep empty bottles and things there, so people are always coming and going.

Besides, I was tired. I had had a very busy morning, helping the men bring in a lot of cases of beer, and running into the saloon to talk to Fred and generally looking after things. So I was just dozing off again, when I heard a voice say, 'Well, he's ugly enough!' Then I knew that they were talking about me.

I have never disguised it from myself, and nobody has ever disguised it from me, that I am not a handsome dog. Even mother never thought me beautiful. She was no Gladys Cooper herself, but she never hesitated to criticize my appearance. In fact, I have yet to meet anyone who did. The first thing strangers say about me is, 'What an ugly dog!'

I don't know what I am. I have a bulldog kind of a face, but the rest of me is terrier. I have a long tail which sticks straight up in the air. My hair is wiry. My eyes are brown. I am jet black, with a white chest. I once overheard Fred saying that I was a Gorgonzola cheese-hound, and I have generally found Fred reliable in his statements.

When I found that I was under discussion, I opened my eyes. Master was standing there, looking down at me, and by his side the man who had just said I was ugly enough. The man was a thin man, about the age of a barman and smaller than a policeman. He had patched brown shoes and black trousers.

'But he's got a sweet nature,' said master.

This was true, luckily for me. Mother always said, 'A dog without influence or private means, if he is to make his way in the world, must have either good looks or amiability.' But, according to her, I overdid it. 'A dog,' she used to say, 'can have a good heart, without chumming with every Tom, Dick, and Harry he meets. Your behaviour is sometimes quite un-doglike.' Mother prided herself on being a one-man dog. She kept herself to herself, and wouldn't kiss anybody except master – not even Fred.

Now, I'm a mixer. I can't help it. It's my nature. I like men. I like the taste of their boots, the smell of their legs, and the sound of their voices. It may be weak of me, but a man has only to speak to me and a sort of thrill goes right down my spine and sets my tail wagging.

I wagged it now. The man looked at me rather distantly. He didn't pat me. I suspected – what I afterwards found to be the case – that he was shy, so I jumped up at him to put him at his ease. Mother growled again. I felt that she did not approve.

'Why, he's took quite a fancy to you already,' said master.

The man didn't say a word. He seemed to be brooding on something. He was one of those silent men. He reminded me of Joe, the old dog down the street at the grocer's shop, who lies at the door all day, blinking and not speaking to anybody.

Master began to talk about me. It surprised me, the way he praised me. I hadn't a suspicion he admired me so much. From what he said you would have thought I had won prizes and ribbons at the Crystal Palace. But the man didn't seem to be impressed. He kept on saying nothing.

When master had finished telling him what a wonderful dog I was till I blushed, the man spoke.

'Less of it,' he said. 'Half a crown is my bid, and if he was an angel from on high you couldn't get another ha'penny out of me. What about it?'

A thrill went down my spine and out at my tail, for of course I saw now what was happening. The man wanted to buy me and take me away. I looked at master hopefully.

'He's more like a son to me than a dog,' said master, sort of wistful.

'It's his face that makes you feel that way,' said the man, unsympathetically. 'If you had a son that's just how he would look. Half a crown is my offer, and I'm in a hurry.'

'All right,' said master, with a sigh, 'though it's giving him away, a valuable dog like that. Where's your half-crown?'

The man got a bit of rope and tied it round my neck.

I could hear mother barking advice and telling me to be a credit to the family, but I was too excited to listen.

'Good-bye mother,' I said. 'Good-bye, master. Good-bye Fred. Good-bye everybody. I'm off to see life. The Shy Man has bought me for half a crown. Wow!'

I kept running round in circles and shouting, till the man gave me a kick and told me to stop it.

So I did.

I don't know where we went, but it was a long way. I had never been off our street before in my life and I didn't know the whole world was half as big as that. We walked on and on, the man jerking at my rope whenever I wanted to stop and look at anything. He wouldn't even let me pass the time of the day with dogs we met.

When we had gone about a hundred miles and were just going to turn in at a dark doorway, a policeman suddenly stopped the man. I could feel by the way the man pulled at my rope and tried to hurry on that he didn't want to speak to the policeman. The more I saw of the man, the more I saw how shy he was.

'Hi!' said the policeman, and we had to stop.

'I've got a message for you, old pal,' said the policeman. 'It's from the Board of Health. They told me to tell you you needed a change of air. See?'

'All right!' said the man.

'And take it as soon as you like. Else you'll find you'll get it given you. See?'

I looked at the man with a good deal of respect. He was evidently someone important, if they worried so about his health.

'I'm going down to the country tonight,' said the man.

The policeman seemed pleased.

'That's a bit of luck for the country,' he said. 'Don't go changing your mind.'

And we walked on, and went in at the dark doorway, and climbed about a million stairs and went into a room that smelt of rats. The man sat down and swore a little, and I sat and looked at him.

Presently I couldn't keep it in any longer.

'Do we live here?' I said. 'Is it true we're going to the country? Wasn't that policeman a good sort? Don't you like policemen? I knew lots of policemen at the public-house. Are there any other dogs here? What is there for dinner? What's in that cupboard? When are you going to take me out for another run? May I go out and see if I can find a cat?'

'Stop that yelping,' he said.

'When we go to the country, where shall we live? Are you going to be caretaker at a house? Fred's father is a caretaker at a big house in Kent. I've heard Fred talk about it. You didn't meet Fred when you came to the public-house, did you? You would like Fred. I like Fred. Mother likes Fred. We all like Fred.'

I was going to tell him a lot more about Fred, who had always been one of my warmest friends, when he suddenly got hold of a stick and walloped me with it.

'You keep quiet when you're told,' he said.

He really was the shyest man I had ever met. It seemed to hurt him to be spoken to. However, he was the boss, and I had to humour him, so I didn't say any more.

We went down to the country that night, just as the man had told the policeman we would. I was all worked up, for I had heard so much about the country from Fred that I had always wanted to go there. Fred used to go off on a motor-bicycle sometimes to spend the night with his father in Kent, and once he brought back a squirrel with him, which I thought was for me to eat, but mother said no. 'The first thing a dog has to learn,' mother used often to say, 'is that the whole world wasn't created for him to eat.'

It was quite dark when we got to the country, but the man seemed to know where to go. He pulled at my rope, and we began to walk along a road with no people in it at all. We walked on and on, but it was all so new to me that I forgot how tired I was. I could feel my mind broadening with every step I took.

Every now and then we would pass a very big house, which looked as if it was empty, but I knew that there was a caretaker inside, because of Fred's father. These big houses belong to very rich people, but they don't want to live in them till the summer, so they put in caretakers, and the caretakers have a dog to keep off burglars. I wondered if that was what I had been brought here for.

'Are you going to be a caretaker?' I asked the man.

'Shut up,' he said.

So I shut up.

After we had been walking a long time, we came to a cottage. A man came out. My man seemed to know him, for he called him Bill. I was quite surprised to see the man was not at all shy with Bill. They seemed very friendly.

'Is that him?' said Bill, looking at me.

'Bought him this afternoon,' said the man.

'Well,' said Bill, 'he's ugly enough. He looks fierce. If you want a dog, he's the sort of dog you want. But what do you want one for? It seems to me it's a lot of trouble to take, when there's no need of any trouble at all. Why not do what I've always wanted to do? What's wrong with just fixing the dog, same as it's always done, and walking in and helping yourself?'

'I'll tell you what's wrong,' said the man. 'To start with, you can't get at the dog and fix him except by day, when they let him out. At night he's shut up inside the house. And suppose you do fix him during the day, what happens then? Either the bloke gets another before night, or else he sits up all night with a gun. It isn't like as if these blokes was ordinary blokes. They're down here to look after the house. That's their job, and they don't take any chances.'

It was the longest speech I had ever heard the man make, and it seemed to impress Bill. He was quite humble.

'I didn't think of that,' he said. 'We'd best start in to train this tyke at once.'

Mother often used to say, when I went on about wanting to go out into the world and see life, 'You'll be sorry when you do. The world isn't all bones and liver.'

18

And I hadn't been living with the man and Bill in their cottage long before I found out how right she was.

It was the man's shyness that made all the trouble. It seemed as if he hated to be taken notice of.

It started on my very first night at the cottage. I had fallen asleep in the kitchen, tired out after all the excitement of the day and the long walks I had had, when something woke me with a start. It was somebody scratching at the window, trying to get in.

Well, I ask you, I ask any dog, what would you have done in my place? Ever since I was old enough to listen, mother had told me over and over again what I must do in a case like this. It is the A B C of a dog's education. 'If you are in a room and you hear anyone trying to get in,' mother used to say, 'bark. It may be someone who has business there, or it may not. Bark first, and inquire afterwards. Dogs were made to be heard and not seen.'

I lifted my head and yelled. I have a good, deep voice, due to a hound strain in my pedigree, and at the public-house, when there was a full moon, I have often had people leaning out of the windows and saying things all down the street. I took a deep breath and let it go.

'Man!' I shouted. 'Bill! Man! Come quick! Here's a burglar getting in!'

Then somebody struck a light, and it was the man himself. He had come in through the window.

He picked up a stick, and he walloped me. I couldn't

understand it. I couldn't see where I had done the wrong thing. But he was the boss, so there was nothing to be said.

If you'll believe me, that same thing happened every night. Every single night! And sometimes twice or three times before morning. And every time I would bark my loudest, and the man would strike a light and wallop me. The thing was baffling. I couldn't possibly have mistaken what mother had said to me. She said it too often for that. Bark! Bark! Bark! It was the main plank of her whole system of education. And yet, here I was, getting walloped every night for doing it.

I thought it out till my head ached, and finally I got it right. I began to see that mother's outlook was narrow. No doubt, living with a man like master at the public-house, a man without a trace of shyness in his composition, barking was all right. But circumstances alter cases. I belonged to a man who was a mass of nerves, who got the jumps if you spoke to him. What I had to do was to forget the training I had had from mother, sound as it no doubt was as a general thing, and to adapt myself to the needs of the particular man who had happened to buy me. I had tried mother's way, and all it had brought me was walloping, so now I would think for myself.

So next night, when I heard the window go, I lay there without a word, though it went against all my better feelings. I didn't even growl. Someone came in and moved about in the dark, with a lantern, but, though I smelt that it was the man, I didn't ask him a single question. And presently the man lit a light and came over to me and gave me a pat, which was a thing he had never done before.

'Good dog!' he said. 'Now you can have this.'

And he let me lick out the saucepan in which the dinner had been cooked.

After that, we got on fine. Whenever I heard anyone at the window I just kept curled up and took no notice, and every time I got a bone or something good. It was easy, once you had got the hang of things.

It was about a week after that the man took me out one morning, and we walked a long way till we turned in at some big gates and went along a very smooth road till we came to a great house, standing all by itself in the middle of a whole lot of country. There was a big lawn in front of it, and all round there were fields and trees, and at the back a great wood.

The man rang a bell, and the door opened, and an old man came out.

'Well?' he said, not very cordially.

'I thought you might want to buy a good watchdog,' said the man.

'Well, that's queer, your saying that,' said the caretaker. 'It's a coincidence. That's exactly what I do want to buy. I was just thinking of going along and trying to get one. My old dog picked up something this morning that he oughtn't to have, and he's dead, poor feller.'

'Poor feller,' said the man. 'Found an old bone with phosphorus on it, I guess.'

'What do you want for this one?'

'Five shillings.'

'Is he a good watchdog?'

'He's a grand watchdog.'

'He looks fierce enough.'

'Ah!'

So the caretaker gave the man his five shillings, and the man went off and left me.

At first the newness of everything and the un-accustomed smells and getting to know the caretaker, who was a nice old man, prevented my missing the man, but as the day went on and I began to realize that he'd gone and would never come back, I got very depressed. I pattered all over the house, whining. It was a most interesting house, bigger than I thought a house could possibly be, but it couldn't cheer me up. You may think it strange that I should pine for the man, after all the wallopings he had given me, and it is odd, when you come to think of it. But dogs are dogs, and they are built like that. By the time it was evening I was thoroughly miserable. I found a shoe and an old clothes-brush in one of the rooms, but could eat nothing. I just sat and moped.

It's a funny thing, but it seems as if it always happens that just when you are feeling most miserable, something nice happens. As I sat there, there came from outside the sound of a motor-bicycle, and somebody shouted.

It was dear old Fred, my old pal Fred, the best old boy that ever stepped. I recognized his voice in a second, and I was scratching at the door before the old man had time to get up out of his chair.

Well, well, well! That was a pleasant surprise! I ran five times round the lawn without stopping, and then I came back and jumped up at him.

'What are you doing here, Fred?' I said. 'Is this caretaker your father? Have you seen the rabbits in the wood? How long are you going to stop? How's mother? I like the country. Have you come all the way from the public-house? I'm living here now. Your father gave five shillings for me. That's twice as much as I was worth when I saw you last.'

'Why, it's young Nigger!' That was what they called me at the saloon. 'What are you doing here? Where did you get this dog, father?'

'A man sold him to me this morning. Poor old Bob got poisoned. This one ought to be just as good a watchdog. He barks loud enough.'

'He should be. His mother is the best watchdog in London. This cheese-hound used to belong to the boss. Funny him getting down here.'

We went into the house and had supper. And after supper we sat and talked. Fred was only down for the night, he said, because the boss wanted him back next day.

'And I'd sooner have my job, than yours, dad,' he said. 'Of all the lonely places! I wonder you aren't scared of burglars.'

'I've my shot-gun, and there's the dog. I might be scared if it wasn't for him, but he kind of gives me confidence. Old Bob was the same. Dogs are a comfort in the country.'

'Get many tramps here?'

'I've only seen one in two months, and that's the feller who sold me the dog here.'

As they were talking about the man, I asked Fred if he knew him. They might have met at the public-house, when the man was buying me from the boss.

'You would like him,' I said. 'I wish you could have met.'

'What's he growling at?' asked Fred. 'Think he heard something?'

The old man laughed.

'He wasn't growling. He was talking in his sleep. You're nervous, Fred. It comes of living in the city.'

'Well, I am. I like this place in the daytime, but it gives me the pip at night. It's so quiet. How you can stand it here all the time, I can't understand. Two nights of it would have me seeing things.'

His father laughed.

'If you feel like that, Fred, you had better take the gun to bed with you. I shall be quite happy without it.'

'I will,' said Fred. 'I'll take six if you've got them.'

And after that they went upstairs. I had a basket in the hall, which had belonged to Bob, the dog who had got poisoned. It was a comfortable basket, but I was so excited at having met Fred again that I couldn't sleep.

Besides, there was a smell of mice somewhere, and I had to move around, trying to place it.

I was just sniffing at a place in the wall, when I heard a scratching noise. At first I thought it was the mice working in a different place, but, when I listened, I found that the sound came from the window. Somebody was doing something to it from the outside.

If it had been mother, she would have lifted the roof off right there, and so should I, if it hadn't been for what the man had taught me. I didn't think it possible that this could be the man come back, for he had gone away and said nothing about ever seeing me again. But I didn't bark. I stopped where I was and listened. And presently the window came open, and somebody began to climb in.

I gave a good sniff, and I knew it was the man.

I was so delighted that for a moment I nearly forgot myself and shouted with joy, but I remembered in time how shy he was, and stopped myself. But I ran to him and jumped up quite quietly, and he told me to lie down. I was disappointed that he didn't seem more pleased to see me. I lay down.

It was very dark, but he had brought a lantern with him, and I could see him moving about the room, picking things up and putting them in a bag which he had brought with him. Every now and then he would stop and listen, and then he would start moving round again. He was very quick about it, but very quiet. It was plain that he didn't want Fred or his father to come down and find him.

I kept thinking about this peculiarity of his while I watched him. I suppose, being chummy myself, I find it hard to understand that everybody else in the world isn't chummy too. Of course, my experience at the public-house had taught me that men are just as different from each other as dogs. If I chewed master's shoe, for instance, he used to kick me; but if I chewed Fred's, Fred would tickle me under the ear. And, similarly, some men are shy and some men are mixers. I quite appreciated that, but I couldn't help feeling that the man carried shyness to a point where it became morbid. And he didn't give himself a chance to cure himself of it. That was the point. Imagine a man hating to meet people so much that he never visited their houses till the middle of the night, when they were in bed and asleep. It was silly. Shyness has always been something so outside my nature that I suppose I have never really been able to look at it sympathetically. I have always held the view that you can get over it if you make an effort. The trouble with the man was that he wouldn't make an effort. He went out of his way to avoid meeting people.

I was fond of the man. He was the sort of person you never got to know very well, but we had been together for quite a while, and I wouldn't have been a dog if I hadn't got attached to him.

As I sat and watched him creep about the room, it suddenly came to me that here was a chance of doing him a real good turn in spite of himself. Fred was upstairs, and Fred, as I knew by experience, was the easiest man to get along with in the world. Nobody could be shy with Fred. I felt that if only I could bring him and the man together, they would get along splendidly, and it would teach the man not to be silly and avoid people. It would help to give him the confidence which he needed. I had seen him with Bill, and I knew that he could be perfectly natural and easy when he liked.

It was true that the man might object at first, but after a while he would see that I had acted simply for his good, and would be grateful.

The difficulty was, how to get Fred down without scaring the man. I knew that if I shouted he wouldn't wait, but would be out of the window and away before Fred could get there. What I had to do was to go to Fred's room, explain the whole situation quietly to him, and ask him to come down and make himself pleasant.

The man was far too busy to pay any attention to me. He was kneeling in a corner with his back to me, putting something in his bag. I seized the opportunity to steal softly from the room.

Fred's door was shut, and I could hear him snoring. I scratched gently, and then harder, till I heard the snores stop. He got out of bed and opened the door.

'Don't make a noise,' I whispered. 'Come on downstairs. I want you to meet a friend of mine.'

At first he was quite peevish.

'What's the idea,' he said, 'coming and spoiling a man's beauty-sleep? Get out.'

He actually started to go back into the room.

'No, honestly, Fred,' I said, 'I'm not fooling you. There is a man downstairs. He got in through the window. I want you to meet him. He's very shy, and I think it will do him good to have a chat with you.'

'What are you whining about?' Fred began, and then he broke off suddenly and listened. We could both hear the man's footsteps as he moved about.

Fred jumped back into the room. He came out carrying something. He didn't say any more, but started to go downstairs, very quiet, and I went after him.

There was the man, still putting things in his bag. I was just going to introduce Fred, when Fred, the silly ass, gave a great yell.

I could have bitten him.

'What did you want to do that for, you chump?' I said. 'I told you he was shy. Now you've scared him.'

He certainly had. The man was out of the window quicker than you would have believed possible. He just flew out. I called after him that it was only Fred and me, but at that moment a gun went off with a tremendous bang, so he couldn't have heard me.

I was pretty sick about it. The whole thing had gone wrong. Fred seemed to have lost his head entirely. He was behaving like a perfect ass. Naturally the man had been frightened with him carrying on in that way. I jumped out of the window to see if I could find the man and explain, but he was gone. Fred jumped out after me, and nearly squashed me.

It was pitch dark out there. I couldn't see a thing. But I knew the man could not have gone far, or I should have heard him. I started to sniff round on the chance of picking up his trail. It wasn't long before I struck it.

Fred's father had come down now, and they were running about. The old man had a light. I followed the trail, and it ended at a large cedar-tree, not far from the house. I stood underneath it and looked up, but of course I could not see anything.

'Are you up there?' I shouted. 'There's nothing to be scared at. It was only Fred. He's an old pal of mine. He works at the place where you bought me. His gun went off by accident. He won't hurt you.'

There wasn't a sound. I began to think I must have made a mistake.

'He's got away,' I heard Fred say to his father and, just as he said it I caught a faint sound of someone moving in the branches above me.

'No he hasn't!' I shouted. 'He's up this tree.'

'I believe the dog's found him, dad!'

'Yes, he's up here. Come along and meet him.'

Fred came to the foot of the tree.

'You up there,' he said, 'come along down.'

Not a sound from the tree.

'It's all right,' I explained, 'he is up there, but he's very shy. Ask him again.'

'All right,' said Fred. 'Stay there if you want to. But I'm going to shoot off this gun into the branches just for fun.'

And then the man started to come down. As soon as he touched the ground I jumped up at him.

'This is fine!' I said. 'Here's my friend Fred. You'll like him.'

But it wasn't any good. They didn't get along together at all. They hardly spoke. The man went into the house, and Fred went after him, carrying his gun. And when they got into the house it was just the same. The man sat in one chair, and Fred sat in another, and after a long time some men came in a motor-car, and the man went away with them. He didn't say good-bye to me.

When he had gone, Fred and his father made a great fuss of me. I couldn't understand it. Men are so odd. The man wasn't a bit pleased that I had brought him and Fred together, but Fred seemed as if he couldn't do enough for me for having introduced him to the man. However, Fred's father produced some cold ham – my favourite dish – and gave me quite a lot of it, so I stopped worrying over the thing. As mother used to say, 'Don't bother your head about what doesn't concern you. The only thing a dog need concern himself with is the bill-of-fare. Eat your bun, and don't make yourself busy about other people's affairs.' Mother's was in some ways a narrow outlook, but she had a great fund of sterling common sense.

The Fugitives

The shadows were lengthening across the terrace, but the thick beech hedge that divided it from the next garden made a sheltered corner, and Lucian, sitting on the broad stone bench that followed the curve of the hedge, did not really need the striped native blanket round his legs. But he knew that if he threw it off, Marcipor, his father's body-slave, who had carried him out there, would fuss like an old woman.

He leaned sideways, frowning in concentration at the lump of clay on the broad raised bench-end – Marcipor had begged it for him from his friend who worked for a potter by the East Gate – which he was trying to work up into the likeness of a sleeping hound. The trouble was that he couldn't remember quite how a hound's muzzle went when it was flattened by resting across the paws. He must notice, next time he saw Syrius lying beside Father's feet in the evening.

The little spring wind blowing across the cantonment brought the thin silver crowing of trumpets from the fort; brought, too, the sound of boys' voices and the barking of a dog. The Senior Centurion's house was the last in the cantonment, and beyond the terrace wall open land dropped gently to the slow silver loop of the river. And looking up from the clay hound, Lucian could see three boys and a half-grown sheep-dog pup racing across the hillside, the boys whooping as they ran, the pup circling ahead of them with streaming ears and tail.

Lucian could remember how it felt to run like that. He was twelve now, and he had been seven when the strange sickness came; other children had had it, too, and mostly they had died. Lucian hadn't died, but when the sickness passed, he had not been able to run any more.

The boys and the dog had disappeared now, and he returned to the clay hound. Despite his uncertainty about the muzzle, it seemed to him that it had begun to look like Syrius, and also that there was a liveness about it. Not just cold clay any more but with something of Syrius in it – or maybe something of himself. It was not very long ago that he had discovered that he could make clay do that; and it still surprised him and gave him a rather odd sensation in the pit of his stomach.

A brushing and crashing in the midst of the beech hedge made him look up again, twisting round on the bench, just in time to see a man diving through. A man who half fell, gathered himself again, and stumbled forward a pace or two, then checked, snatching a glance behind him at the torn twigs and scatter of last year's brown leaves that marked the way he had come.

Lucian gave a sharp gasp, and the intruder whipped round, his hand leaping to the dagger at his belt, and their eyes met.

The odd thing was that the boy was not in the least frightened, and after that first startled moment, he simply sat and looked at the man, while the stranger stood and stared back out of strained grey eyes in a very young grey face. Rough hair clung wetly to his sweating forehead, and his breast panted in and out like the flanks of a hunted animal.

Lucian was the first to speak. 'What is it? Are you running away from something? – A runaway slave?'

The man swallowed thickly, and steadied his sobbing breath, and for an instant, unlikely as it seemed, there was a flicker of reckless laughter in his face. 'You could call it that.'

'And they are after you?'

The man nodded.

But Lucian was noticing that the tattered tunic with the brown of last year's leaves clinging to it was the regulation red cloth tunic that the Auxiliaries wore under their leather jerkins. 'It's the Eagles you're running away from! You're a deserter!'

'Right second time – and they're hunting the cantonment for me.'

Scorn blazed up in Lucian. 'I hope they catch you and drag you back!'

'I'm not going back. I've had enough,' the deserter said slowly. 'I'll die first – and so will you!' He was close to Lucian now, and the point of the dagger just kissed against the boy's throat.

Lucian looked at the hand that held it, and up the arm, and came again to the grey, desperate face. His mouth was dry, and he licked his lower lip.

'Now listen. You haven't seen anybody pass this way.'

'I have! And you can't stop me telling as soon as you're gone!'

The deserter said, 'Not unless I kill you now, and I don't want to do that if I can help it. But if I am retaken, I'll live long enough to escape once more, and then I shall come and kill you.'

'I'll shout!' Lucian said, desperately. 'There are people quite near!' And all the while he was listening, listening for the sounds of the hunt.

'They'd need to be very near to come before this blade was in your throat! It is too late for shouting; it's too late to run now, too; the time for running was when I first broke through the hedge.'

'I – if you kill me now, they'll crucify you when they do catch you.' Lucian heard his own voice not sounding quite like his own. 'And if you don't, I shall tell which way you went, and you can talk big, but you won't get your chance to escape again. That's bairn's talk.'

For the first time he saw a flicker of uncertainty in the man's eyes and slowly the dagger was withdrawn a thumb-nail's breadth from his throat. 'If I take this away, will you promise not to bolt?' the man said, in a changed tone.

'Yes.' Not for anything in the world would he have admitted that he couldn't.

The dagger was withdrawn and sheathed. The man hesitated still an instant and glanced back again the way he had come, listening for sounds of the hunt. Then he seemed to come to a decision and spoke quickly and urgently. 'I've twisted my ankle and I'm just about done, or I'd not be telling you this, but it seems I've not much choice. And I shan't have time to tell you more than once, so listen . . . I'm carrying secret dispatches for Caesar – so secret and so deadly that to get them past our enemies, I've had to play the deserter. They know nothing of that up at the fort; to them I'm just a deserter like any other, and if they catch up with me –'

He broke off with a small, one-shouldered shrug.

Lucian's heart, which had not quickened much, even with the dagger at his throat, fell over itself and began to pound like a runner's at the end of a race. 'If they catch up with you?'

'I can't tell you. It would – be disaster for the whole province. I can't tell you any more.'

And at that moment the little wind brought the first rumour of the sounds they had both been listening for: a small smother of sounds that if they had been made by hounds instead of men, would have been a pack giving tongue on a hot scent.

Despite the drubbing of his heart, Lucian's head had started to feel cold and clear, as though it were set far above the level of what was happening around him. 'Get under the bench! I'll pull the blanket over the front of it, and if you get close up this end, behind my legs –'

The man looked at him for one instant, as though testing for a trap, and then in another way, as though he were puzzled, maybe, by the blanket and the way the boy had never attempted to get up or dive clear. Then he nodded, and without a word dropped on hands and knees and was gone under cover.

Lucian dragged the rug from his legs in frantic haste, and flung the free half of it out along the bench so that it trailed down in front and made a small dark hiding-place for the desperate man he could feel crouching there. Then he began with great care and concentration to do something – he never knew what – about the way the hound's muzzle was pressed up by the paws.

Everything had happened at racing speed, and now there was a sudden blankness of nothing happening at all, and all the while he was terrified that Syrius, who was in the kitchen hoping for a bone, would come trotting down the garden and smell the stranger under the bench, or that Marcipor would come and fetch him in.

And then the search-party was in the very next garden, and the old garden-slave was scolding like an angry hen because somebody's great feet were in his herb patch. Someone only a few feet away called, 'Sir! Here's a broken place in the hedge; he's gone this way!'

36

and there was a sharp exclamation and footsteps on gravel, and then:

'No, not through the hedge, too, you fool! It's the Pilus Prior's garden. Over the wall at the bottom,' and the half-running tramp of feet going down beyond the hedge.

Lucian caught a deep breath, and looked up from the little clay figure as half a dozen legionaries led by a young Centurion came scrambling over the terrace wall.

The Centurion saw the boy on the bench and called out to him almost before both feet were on the terrace: 'There's been a man through here. Which way did he go?'

'What man? There hasn't been any man,' Lucian's voice wobbled a little and the Centurion, a cheerful-looking, freckled individual, came over to him while his men scattered at once to search the garden.

'Then why are you looking as though you'd seen a ghost?' he asked.

Lucian managed a grin. 'Six – no, seven ghosts. You and your lot made me jump. I didn't hear you coming.'

'Fair enough. Look now, we're hunting a deserter, and we know he came this way. Where did he go?'

'No one has been through the garden while I've been out here.'

'How long is that?'

'An hour or more.'

'And no one passed?'

'I told you!'

The Centurion jerked his chin towards the broken place in the hedge. 'Who made that, then?'

'That?' Lucian gazed blankly in the direction indicated.

'Gap in the hedge.'

'Oh that! Syrius our dog made it. They throw out their meat bones because it's good for the roses, and he's always breaking through.'

The Centurion eyed him consideringly, and was silent a moment.

'Don't you believe me?' Lucian said, as haughtily as he could manage. 'My father is Lucius Lycinius, the Pilus Prior of the Legion! Do you d–dare to think I'd go hiding a deserter?'

The Centurion threw back his head with a crack of laughter. 'Roma Dea! I'd know you for the Old Man's son anywhere, when you put on that tone – even if I hadn't known this was his garden . . . But we're searching all this quarter till we find him. He twisted an ankle dropping over the bath-house wall, and he was going as lame as a duck when we lost him. He can't have – got – far.'

His voice trailed off awkwardly, and Lucian realized that the friendly freckle-faced young Centurion knew about him, had probably known all along, and was wishing that he hadn't said that about being lame as a duck and not getting far.

38

He had always hated strangers knowing about him not being able to walk. He hated it now. He felt shamed and a little sick and in the usual way of things he would have glared at the young Centurion to show how much he didn't care; but this time it didn't matter whether he cared or not; all that mattered was to keep them from discovering the man under the bench. And if he could hold the Centurion here standing right against the bench while his men finished their search, they would be less likely to go peering under it.

'Perhaps he's managed to hide in one of the market carts,' he suggested.

'The carts are being checked. Any sign, Rufrius?'

'Not yet, sir.' The shout came back, slightly muffled from among tangled rose and elder bushes that shut off all view of the house.

'Push on farther up that way.'

Lucian searched desperately for something else to say, and found it. 'Why did he desert?'

The Centurion shrugged. 'There are always a few deserters among the Auxiliaries at this time of year. Maybe the homesickness catches them more sharply in the springtime. Poor stupid devils. Even if he's not caught, there's not much life for a deserter; you can't spend all your life running away.'

Lucian gave a little shiver, and covered it by saying, 'It gets cold still, once the sun is behind the hills.'

The Centurion nodded. 'Hadn't you better have that blanket round you?'

'No!' said Lucian quickly, and then, 'It makes my legs stronger to have the air all round them.'

'Ah well, that's the way then,' the Centurion said bracingly. 'You get them good and strong, and we'll have you in the Legion yet.' His eyes were with his men among the bushes; he hitched at his sword-belt, in another instant he would have gone to join them.

And then Lucian heard the sound that he had been dreading. Syrius had winded strangers and was baying his head off in the kitchen quarters; the baying loudened and changed tempo as a door was opened and he could hear Marcipor cursing. Another moment and the great hound would come flying down from the house. He knew legionaries and would not bother much about them once he saw what they were, but a man with the hunted smell on him, hiding under the bench . . .

One blunt stab of hopelessness shot through Lucian. The affair was out of his hands now; only the gods could hold back the terrible thing from happening. In desperation, with no time to think, he did the one thing that was left. He made a sacrifice to the gods. It was an odd sacrifice, but strong, for it meant giving up old dreams that he had not known until that instant he was still clinging on to; it meant doing the hardest and bravest thing he had ever done in his life. He caught the young Centurion's eye in the instant before he turned away, and managed a grin. 'Tell that to the wild geese! My head works well enough, it's only my legs that don't and I've got sense enough to know there's not much room for you in the Legions if you can't walk.'

Syrius and Marcipor appeared where the path curved through the bushes, the slave clinging to the bronze-studded collar of the huge hound who dragged forward, snarling, his hackles raised in a great comb along his back.

Marcipor checked as the Centurion went striding to meet him, and inquired in the coolly respectful tone that could be more blighting than the Pilus Prior's when he chose, whether it was by his Master's orders that half the Legion was in his garden.

Lucian could not hear properly what passed after that, for the two men spoke together quietly, and they were a little way off. But Syrius had stopped snarling, and he saw Marcipor let go the hound's collar and give him an open-palmed slap on the rump to send him back to the house.

Syrius hesitated an instant, looking back, and Lucian, his mouth dry and the palms of his hands sweating, did not dare to look at him direct, lest that should bring him over. Then out of the corner of his eye he saw the hound look away, his ears suddenly pricked, and knew that in the nick of time his father had turned the corner of the street. Syrius always heard him as he turned that corner, every evening. An instant later the hound gave a pleased bark, and went bounding back towards the house.

Relief broke over Lucian in a wave, and he scarcely knew what was happening in the next few moments, until suddenly the search was over, and the Legionaries were going. The Centurion checked beside him in passing, and said, 'My legs are all right, but maybe my head's not so good. I'm sorry we'll not be having you in the Legion.'

Then they were gone, but almost before Lucian could draw breath the next danger was there to be faced, as Marcipor came along the terrace, saying, 'Time you were indoors.'

'No!' Lucian said. 'Not just yet, Marcipor. It feels so good out here after being shut in all the winter.' Then, as the big grey-haired slave hesitated, 'Listen – there's Father calling for you.'

'I didn't hear him.'

'I'm sure I did. Please, Marcipor!'

'Very well, if you have the blanket round you again. Just while I get the Commander out of his harness and see to his bath.'

Lucian hardly knew how to bear it as the slave, still fussing, pulled the blanket back into place and tucked it in. He only had to stoop just a little lower, he only had to look back once as he went up towards the house . . .

But neither of these things happened and in a little while, when the last sounds of the hunt had died away, the man who carried Caesar's dispatches was crouching with his shoulders propped against the bench, rubbing his swollen ankle to ease the stiffness, and pulling in slow gasps of air as though he had been half stifled in his hiding-place. 'That was valiantly done. Do you know, I was wondering, when I crawled under that bench, whether I was crawling into a trap,' he said at last.

'But you had told me about the secret dispatches.'

'Och yes – the dispatches for Caesar.' The man looked up with a wry flicker of something that might have been laughter.

'You must go,' Lucian said. 'You can hide among the rough stuff under the terrace until full dusk, and then make for the river woods. Marcipor will be out soon to carry me back to the house.' He never noticed that he did not mind this man whom he had hidden from the search-party knowing about him.

The man had got up, wincing as his ankle took the strain. 'Like our good friend the Centurion, I'm sorry the Legion will be having to do without you,' he said. 'Maybe it's the Legion's loss.'

'Oh, I don't suppose I'd have made much of a soldier anyway – not like my father.'

'I – wonder.' The young man put out a forefinger and touched the little clay hound. 'One thing I will tell you: maybe you would not have made as good a soldier as your father, but I am very sure your father could not make a lump of potter's clay breathe warm and heavy like a sleeping hound.'

He turned towards the low terrace wall, swung a leg over, and dropped from sight.

Lucian heard the grunt of pain as he landed, and sat

43

looking at the place where he had been, suddenly very tired. He picked up the little hound, but the clay was getting dry. He couldn't work it much more, and he thought he knew now what was wrong with the muzzle. He would keep it, all the same; it was part of something very important. But as soon as he could get some more clay he would make another hound, or maybe something else. And he knew that it would be better than this one.

Somehow he did not think much about Caesar's dispatches. It wasn't until years later that he understood that he had never quite believed that story, and it was simply because the man was being hunted, that he had hidden him.

The deserter crouched among the docks and hazel-scrub under the terrace wall, waiting for the light to go.

He had stuck two years of the Auxiliaries – two years out of twenty-five – and for most of them he had not even been able to remember what had made him join; unless it was simply that the chieftain his grandfather had been so determined that he should head the young men of their valley when they went down to join the draft. Two years of the rigid discipline, the bullying of the Decurion, the loss of freedom, and today, quite suddenly, it had all been more than he could bear. So he had gone out over the bath-house wall.

If he had not twisted his ankle, he'd have been well into the woods, by now. But what was it the Centurion had said? – 'You can't spend all your life running away.' The boy had been running away too, in his own fashion, but then he had stopped. Sweating in the dark under the bench, the deserter had known when the boy stopped running away.

Below him the river woods were blurring into the twilight.

Probably it would not be death, if he gave himself up of his own accord. It would be flogging; it would be cells and bread-and-water and shame; and when all that was over, the cage of discipline and the bullying Decurion, just as before. But maybe one could make some kind of a fresh start?

He felt in an odd way that he had company on his road, when he got up, stumbling on his wrenched ankle, and turned back towards the fort.

How Mowgli Entered the Wolf Pack

It was seven o'clock of a very warm evening in the Seeonee hills when Father Wolf woke up from his day's rest, scratched himself, yawned, and spread out his paws one after the other to get rid of the sleepy feeling in their tips. Mother Wolf lay with her big grey nose dropped across her four tumbling, squealing cubs, and the moon shone into the mouth of the cave where they all lived.

'Augrh!' said Father Wolf. 'It is time to hunt again.' He was going to spring downhill when a little shadow with a bushy tail crossed the threshold and whined: 'Good Luck go with you, O Chief of the Wolves. And good luck and strong white teeth go with the noble children that they may never forget the hungry in this world.'

It was the jackal – Tabaqui, the Dishlicker – and the wolves of India despise Tabaqui because he runs about making mischief, and telling tales, and eating rags and pieces of leather from the village rubbish heaps. But they are afraid of him too, because Tabaqui, more than anyone else in the jungle, is apt to go mad, and then he forgets that he was ever afraid of anyone, and runs through the forest biting everything in his way. Even the tiger runs and hides when little Tabaqui goes mad, for madness is the most disgraceful thing that can overtake a wild creature. We call it hydrophobia, but they call it dewanee – the madness – and run.

'Enter, then, and look,' said Father Wolf stiffly, 'but there is no food here.'

'For a wolf, no,' said Tabaqui, 'but for so mean a person as myself a dry bone is a good feast. Who are we, the Gidurlog (the jackal people), to pick and choose?' He scuttled to the back of the cave, where he found the bone of a buck with some meat on it, and sat cracking the end merrily.

'All thanks for this good meal,' he said, licking his lips. 'How beautiful are the noble children! How large are their eyes! And so young too! Indeed, indeed, I might have remembered that the children of kings are men from the beginning.'

Now, Tabaqui knew as well as anyone else that there is nothing so unlucky as to compliment children to their faces. It pleased him to see Mother and Father Wolf look uncomfortable.

Tabaqui sat still, rejoicing in the mischief that he had made, and then he said spitefully:

'Shere Khan, the Big One, has shifted his hunting grounds. He will hunt among these hills for the next moon, so he has told me.'

Shere Khan was the tiger who lived near the Waingunga River, twenty miles away.

'He has no right!' Father Wolf began angrily – 'By the Law of the Jungle he has no right to change his quarters without due warning. He will frighten every head of game within ten miles, and I – I have to kill for two, these days.'

'His mother did not call him Lungri (the Lame One) for nothing,' said Mother Wolf quietly. 'He has been lame in one foot from his birth. That is why he has only killed cattle. Now the villagers of the Waingunga are angry with him, and he has come here to make our villagers angry. They will scour the jungle for him when he is far away, and we and our children must run when the grass is set alight. Indeed, we are very grateful to Shere Khan!'

'Shall I tell him of your gratitude?' said Tabaqui.

'Out!' snapped Father Wolf. 'Out and hunt with thy master. Thou hast done harm enough for one night.'

'I go,' said Tabaqui quietly. 'Ye can hear Shere Khan below in the thickets. I might have saved myself the message.'

Father Wolf listened, and below in the valley that ran down to a little river he heard the dry, angry, snarly, sing-song whine of a tiger who has caught nothing and does not care if all the jungle knows it.

'The fool!' said Father Wolf. 'To begin a night's work with that noise! Does he think that our buck are like his fat Waingunga bullocks?'

48

'H'sh. It is neither bullock nor buck he hunts tonight,' said Mother Wolf. 'It is Man.'

The whine had changed to a sort of humming purr that seemed to come from every quarter of the compass. It was the noise that bewilders woodcutters and gypsies sleeping in the open, and makes them run sometimes into the very mouth of the tiger.

'Man!' said Father Wolf, showing all his white teeth. 'Faugh! Are there not enough beetles and frogs in the tanks that he must eat Man, and on our ground too!'

The Law of the Jungle, which never orders anything without a reason, forbids every beast to eat Man except when he is killing to show his children how to kill, and then he must hunt outside the hunting grounds of his pack or tribe. The real reason for this is that man-killing means, sooner or later, the arrival of white men on elephants, with guns, and hundreds of brown men with gongs and rockets and torches. Then everybody in the jungle suffers. The reason the beasts give among themselves is that Man is the weakest and most defenceless of all living things, and it is unsportsmanlike to touch him. They say too – and it is true – that man-eaters become mangy, and lose their teeth.

The purr grew louder, and ended in the full-throated 'Aaarh!' of the tiger's charge.

Then there was a howl – an untigerish howl – from Shere Khan. 'He has missed,' said Mother Wolf. 'What is it?'

Father Wolf ran out a few paces and heard Shere

Khan muttering and mumbling as he tumbled about in the scrub.

'The fool has had no more sense than to jump at a woodcutter's campfire, and has burned his feet,' said Father Wolf with a grunt. 'Tabaqui is with him.'

'Something is coming uphill,' said Mother Wolf, twitching one ear. 'Get ready.'

The bushes rustled a little in the thicket, and Father Wolf dropped with his haunches under him, ready for his leap. Then, if you had been watching, you would have seen the most wonderful thing in the world – the wolf checked in mid-spring. He made his bound before he saw what it was he was jumping at, and then he tried to stop himself. The result was that he shot up straight into the air for four or five feet, landing almost where he left ground.

'Man!' he snapped. 'A man's cub. Look!'

Directly in front of him, holding on by a low branch, stood a naked brown baby who could just walk – as soft and as dimpled a little atom as ever came to a wolf's cave at night. He looked up into Father Wolf's face and laughed.

'Is that a man's cub?' said Mother Wolf. 'I have never seen one. Bring it here.'

A wolf accustomed to moving his own cubs can, if necessary, mouth an egg without breaking it, and though Father Wolf's jaws closed right on the child's back not a tooth even scratched the skin as he laid it down among the cubs.

'How little! How naked, and – how bold!' said Mother Wolf softly. The baby was pushing his way between the cubs to get close to the warm hide. 'Ahai! He is taking his meal with the others. And so this is a man's cub. Now, was there ever a wolf that could boast of a man's cub among her children?'

'I have heard now and again of such a thing, but never in our Pack or in my time,' said Father Wolf. 'He is altogether without hair, and I could kill him with a touch of my foot. But see, he looks up and is not afraid.'

The moonlight was blocked out of the mouth of the cave, for Shere Khan's great square head and shoulders were thrust into the entrance. Tabaqui, behind him, was squeaking: 'My lord, my lord, it went in here!'

'Shere Khan does us great honour,' said Father Wolf but his eyes were very angry. 'What does Shere Khan need?'

'My quarry. A man's cub went this way,' said Shere Khan. 'Its parents have run off. Give it to me.'

Shere Khan had jumped at a woodcutter's campfire, as Father Wolf had said, and was furious from the pain of his burned feet. But Father Wolf knew that the mouth of the cave was too narrow for a tiger to come in by. Even where he was, Shere Khan's shoulders and forepaws were cramped for want of room, as a man's would be if he tried to fight in a barrel.

'The Wolves are a free people,' said Father Wolf. 'They take orders from the Head of the Pack, and not

from any striped cattle-killer. The man's cub is ours –
to kill if we choose.'

'Ye choose and ye do not choose! What talk is this of
choosing? By the bull that I killed, am I to stand nosing
into your dog's den for my fair dues? It is I, Shere
Khan, who speak!'

The tiger's roar filled the cave with thunder. Mother
Wolf shook herself clear of the cubs and sprang forward,
her eyes, like two green moons in the darkness, facing
the blazing eyes of Shere Khan.

'And it is I, Raksha (The Demon), who answers.
The man's cub is mine, Lungri – mine to me! He shall
not be killed. He shall live to run with the Pack and to
hunt with the Pack; and in the end, look you, hunter of
little naked cubs – frog-eater – fish-killer – he shall hunt
thee! Now get hence, or by the Sambhur that I killed
(I eat no starved cattle), back thou goest to thy mother,
burned beast of the jungle, lamer than ever thou camest
into the world! Go!'

Father Wolf looked on amazed. He had almost forgotten the days when he won Mother Wolf in fair fight
from five other wolves, when she ran in the Pack and
was not called The Demon for compliment's sake. Shere
Khan might have faced Father Wolf, but he could not
stand up against Mother Wolf, for he knew that where
he was she had all the advantage of the ground, and
would fight to the death. So he backed out of the cave
mouth, growling, and when he was clear he shouted:

'Each dog barks in his own yard! We will see what

the Pack will say to this fostering of man-cubs. The cub is mine, and to my teeth he will come in the end, O bush-tailed thieves!'

Mother Wolf threw herself down panting among the cubs, and Father Wolf said to her gravely:

'Shere Khan speaks this much truth. The cub must be shown to the Pack. Wilt thou still keep him, Mother?'

'Keep him!' she gasped. 'He came naked, by night, alone and very hungry; yet he was not afraid! Look, he has pushed one of my babies to one side already. And that lame butcher would have killed him and would have run off to the Waingunga while the villagers here hunted through all our lairs in revenge! Keep him? Assuredly, I will keep him. Lie still, little frog. O thou Mowgli – for Mowgli the Frog I will call thee – the time will come when thou wilt hunt Shere Khan as he has hunted thee.'

'But what will our Pack say?' said Father Wolf.

The Law of the Jungle lays down very clearly that any wolf may, when he marries, withdraw from the Pack he belongs to. But as soon as his cubs are old enough to stand on their feet he must bring them to the Pack Council, which is generally held once a month at full moon, in order that the other wolves may identify them. After that inspection the cubs are free to run where they please, and until they have killed their first buck no excuse is accepted if a grown wolf of the Pack kills one of them. The punishment is death where the murderer can be found, and if you think for a minute you will see that this must be so.

Father Wolf waited till his cubs could run a little, and then on the night of the Pack Meeting took them and Mowgli and Mother to the Council Rock – a hill-top covered with stones and boulders where a hundred wolves could hide. Akela, the great grey Lone Wolf, who led all the Pack by strength and cunning, lay out at full length on his rock, and below him sat forty or more wolves of every size and colour, from badger-coloured veterans who could handle a buck alone to young black three-year-olds who thought they could. The Lone Wolf had led them for a year now. He had fallen twice into a wolf trap in his youth and once he had been beaten and left for dead; so he knew the manners and customs of men. There was very little talking at the Rock. The cubs tumbled over each other in the centre of the circle where their mothers and fathers sat, and now and again a senior wolf would go quietly up to a cub, look at him carefully, and return to his place on noiseless feet. Sometimes a mother would push her cub far out into the moonlight to be sure that he had not been overlooked. Akela from his rock would cry: 'Ye know the Law – ye know the Law. Look well, O wolves!' And the anxious mothers would take up the call: 'Look – look well, O Wolves!'

At last – and Mother Wolf's neck bristles lifted as the time came – Father Wolf pushed 'Mowgli the Frog,' as they called him, into the centre, where he sat laughing

55

and playing with some pebbles that glistened in the moonlight.

Akela never raised his head from his paws, but went on with the monotonous cry: 'Look well!'

There was a chorus of deep growls, and a young wolf in his fourth year flung back Shere Khan's question to Akela: 'What have the Free People to do with a man's cub?' Now, the Law of the Jungle lays down that if there is any dispute as to the right of a cub to be accepted by the Pack, he must be spoken for by at least two members of the Pack who are not his father and mother.

'Who speaks for this cub?' said Akela. 'Among the Free People who speaks?' There was no answer and Mother Wolf got ready for what she knew would be her last fight, if things came to fighting.

Then the only other creature who is allowed at the Pack Council – Baloo, the sleepy brown bear who teaches the wolf cubs the Law of the Jungle: Old Baloo, who can come and go where he pleases because he eats only nuts and roots and honey – rose upon his hind quarters and grunted.

'The man's cub – the man's cub?' he said. 'I speak for the man's cub. There is no harm in a man's cub. I have no gift of words, but I speak the truth. Let him run with the Pack, and be entered with the others. I myself will teach him.'

'We need yet another,' said Akela. 'Baloo has spoken, and he is our teacher for the young cubs. Who speaks besides Baloo?'

56

A black shadow dropped down into the circle. It was Bagheera the Black Panther, inky black all over, but with the panther markings showing up in certain lights like the pattern of watered silk. Everybody knew Bagheera, and nobody cared to cross his path; for he was as cunning as Tabaqui, as bold as the wild buffalo, and as reckless as the wounded elephant. But he had a voice as soft as wild honey dripping from a tree, and a skin softer than down.

'O Akela, and ye the Free People,' he purred, 'I have no right in your assembly, but the Law of the Jungle says that if there is a doubt which is not a killing matter in regard to a new cub, the life of that cub may be bought at a price. And the Law does not say who may or may not pay that price. Am I right?'

'Good! Good!' said the young wolves, who are always hungry. 'Listen to Bagheera. The cub can be bought for a price. It is the Law.'

'Knowing that I have no right to speak here, I ask your leave.'

'Speak then,' cried twenty voices.

'To kill a naked cub is shame. Besides, he may make better sport for you when he is grown. Baloo has spoken in his behalf. Now to Baloo's word I will add one bull, and a fat one, newly killed, not half a mile from here, if ye will accept the man's cub according to the Law. Is it difficult?'

There was a clamour of scores of voices, saying: 'What matter? He will die in the winter rains. He will scorch in the sun. What harm can a naked frog do us? Let him run with the Pack. Where is the bull, Bagheera? Let him be accepted.' And then came Akela's deep bay, crying: 'Look well – look well, O Wolves!'

Mowgli was still deeply interested in the pebbles, and he did not notice when the wolves came and looked at him one by one. At last they all went down the hill for the dead bull, and only Akela, Bagheera, Baloo, and Mowgli's own wolves were left. Shere Khan roared still in the night, for he was very angry that Mowgli had not been handed over to him.

'Ay, roar well,' said Bagheera, under his whiskers, 'for the time will come when this naked thing will make thee roar to another tune, or I know nothing of man.'

'It was well done,' said Akela. 'Men and their cubs are very wise. He may be a help in time.'

'Truly, a help in time of need; for none can hope to lead the Pack forever,' said Bagheera.

Akela said nothing. He was thinking of the time that comes to every leader of every pack when his strength goes from him and he gets feebler and feebler, till at last he is killed by the wolves and a new leader comes up – to be killed in his turn.

'Take him away,' he said to Father Wolf, 'and train him as befits one of the Free People.'

And that is how Mowgli was entered into the Seeonee Wolf Pack for the price of a bull and on Baloo's good word.

Spit Nolan

Spit Nolan was a pal of mine. He was a thin lad with a bony face that was always pale, except for two rosy spots on his cheekbones. He had quick brown eyes, short, wiry hair, rather stooped shoulders, and we all knew that he had only one lung. He had had a disease which in those days couldn't be cured, unless you went away to Switzerland, which Spit certainly couldn't afford. He wasn't sorry for himself in any way, and in fact we envied him, because he never had to go to school.

Spit was the champion trolley-rider of Cotton Pocket; that was the district in which we lived. He had a very good balance and sharp wits, and he was very brave, so that these qualities, when added to his skill as a rider, meant that no other boy could ever beat Spit on a trolley – and every lad had one.

Our trolleys were simple vehicles for getting a good ride down hill at a fast speed. To make one you had to get a stout piece of wood about five feet in length and eighteen inches wide. Then you needed four wheels, preferably two pairs, large ones for the back and smaller ones for the front. However, since we bought our wheels from the scrapyard, most trolleys had four odd wheels. Now you had to get a poker and put it in the fire until it was red hot, and then burn a hole through the wood at the front. Usually it would take three or four attempts to get the hole bored through. Through this hole you fitted the giant nut-and-bolt, which acted as a swivel for the steering. Fastened to the nut was a strip of wood, on to which the front axle was secured by bent nails. A piece of rope tied to each end of the axle served for steering. Then a knob of margarine had to be slanced out of the kitchen to grease the wheels and bearings. Next you had to paint a name on it: *Invincible* or *Dreadnought*, though it might be a motto: *Death before Dishonour* or *Labour and Wait*. That done, you then stuck your chest out, opened the back gate, and wheeled your trolley out to face the critical eyes of the world.

Spit spent most mornings trying out new speed gadgets on his trolley, or searching Enry's scrapyard for good wheels. Afternoons he would go off and have a spin down Cemetery Brew. This was a very steep road that led to the cemetery, and it was very popular with trolley-drivers as it was the only macadamized hill for miles around, all the others being cobblestones for horse traffic. Spit used to lie in wait for a coal-cart or other horse-drawn vehicle, then he would hitch *Egdam* to the back to take it up the brew. *Egdam* was a name in memory of a girl called Madge, whom he had once met at Southport Sanatorium, where he had spent three happy weeks. Only I knew the meaning of it, for he had reversed the letters of her name to keep his love a secret.

It was the custom for lads to gather at the street corner on summer evenings and, trolleys parked at hand, discuss trolleying, road surfaces, and also show off any new gadgets. Then, when Spit gave the sign, we used to set off for Cemetery Brew. There was scarcely any evening traffic on the roads in those days, so that we could have a good practice before our evening race. Spit, the unbeaten champion, would inspect every trolley and rider, and allow a start which was reckoned on the size of the wheels and the weight of the rider. He was always the last in the line of starters, though no matter how long a start he gave it seemed impossible to beat him. He knew the road like the palm of his hand, every tiny lump or pothole, and he never came a cropper.

Among us he took things easy, but when occasion asked for it he would go all out. Once he had to meet a challenge from Ducker Smith, the champion of the Engine Row gang. On that occasion Spit borrowed a wheel from the baby's pram, removing the one nearest the wall, so it wouldn't be missed, and confident he could replace it before his mother took baby out. And after fixing it to his trolley he made that ride on what was called the 'belly-down' style – that is, he lay full stretch on his stomach, so as to avoid wind resistance. Although Ducker got away with a flying start he had not that sensitive touch of Spit, and his frequent bumps and swerves lost him valuable inches, so that he lost the race with a good three lengths. Spit arrived home just in time to catch his mother as she was wheeling young Georgie off the doorstep, and if he had not made a dash for it the child would have fallen out as the pram overturned.

It happened that we were gathered at the street corner with our trolleys one evening when Ernie Haddock let out a hiccup of wonder: 'By, chaps, wot's Leslie got?'

We all turned our eyes on Leslie Duckett, the plump son of the local publican. He approached us on a brand-new trolley, propelled by flicks of his foot on the pavement. From a distance the thing had looked impressive, but now, when it came up among us, we were too dumbfounded to speak. Such a magnificent trolley had never been seen! The riding board was of solid oak, almost two inches thick; four new wheels with pneumatic tyres; a brake, a bell, a lamp, and a spotless steering-cord. In front was a plate on which was the name in bold lettering: *The British Queen*.

'It's called after the pub,' remarked Leslie. He tried to edge it away from Spit's trolley, for it made *Egdam* appear horribly insignificant. Voices had been stilled for a minute, but now they broke out.

'Where'd it come from?'

'How much was it?'

'Who made it?'

Leslie tried to look modest. 'My dad had it specially made to measure,' he said, 'by the gaffer of the Holt Engineering Works.'

He was a nice lad, and now he wasn't sure whether to feel proud or ashamed. The fact was, nobody had ever had a trolley made by somebody else. Trolleys were swopped and so on, but no lad had ever owned one that had been made by other hands. We went quiet now, for Spit had calmly turned his attention to it, and was examining *The British Queen* with his expert eye. First he tilted it, so that one of the rear wheels was off the ground, and after giving it a flick of the finger he listened intently with his ear close to the hub.

'A beautiful ball-bearing race,' he remarked, 'it runs like silk.' Next he turned his attention to the body. 'Grand piece of timber, Leslie – though a trifle on the heavy side. It'll take plenty of pulling up a brew.'

'I can pull it,' said Leslie, stiffening.

'You might find it a shade front-heavy,' went on Spit, 'which means it'll be hard on the steering unless you keep it well oiled.'

'It's well made,' said Leslie. 'Eh, Spit?'

Spit nodded. 'Aye, all the bolts are counter-sunk,' he said, 'everything chamfered and fluted off to perfection. But –'

'But what?' asked Leslie.

'Do you want me to tell you?' asked Spit.

'Yes, I do,' answered Leslie.

'Well, it's got none of you in it,' said Spit.

'How do you mean?' says Leslie.

'Well, you haven't so much as given it a single tap with a hammer,' said Spit. 'That trolley will be a stranger to you to your dying day.'

'How come,' said Leslie, 'since I own it?'

Spit shook his head. 'You don't own it,' he said, in a quiet, solemn tone. 'You own nothing in this world except those things you have taken a hand in the making of, or else you've the money to buy them.'

Leslie sat down on *The British Queen* to think this one out. We all sat round, scratching our heads.

'You've forgotten to mention one thing,' said Ernie Haddock to Spit, 'what about the speed?'

'Going down a steep hill,' said Spit, 'she should hold the road well – an' with wheels like that she should certainly be able to shift some.'

'Think she could beat *Egdam*?' ventured Ernie.

'That,' said Spit, 'remains to be seen.'

Ernie gave a shout: 'A challenge race! *The British Queen* versus *Egdam*!'

'Not tonight,' said Leslie. 'I haven't got the proper feel of her yet.'

'What about Sunday morning?' I said.

Spit nodded. 'As good a time as any.'

Leslie agreed. 'By then,' he said in a challenging tone, 'I'll be able to handle her.'

Chattering like monkeys, eating bread, carrots, fruit, and bits of toffee, the entire gang of us made our way along the silent Sunday-morning streets for the big race at Cemetery Brew. We were split into two fairly equal sides.

Leslie, in his serge Sunday suit, walked ahead, with Ernie Haddock pulling *The British Queen*, and a bunch of supporters around. They were optimistic, for Leslie had easily outpaced every other trolley during the week, though as yet he had not run against Spit.

Spit was in the middle of the group behind, and I was pulling *Egdam* and keeping the pace easy, for I wanted Spit to keep fresh. He walked in and out among us with an air of imperturbability that, considering the occasion, seemed almost godlike. It inspired a fanatical confidence in us. It was such that Chick Dale, a curly-headed kid with soft skin like a girl's and a nervous lisp, climbed up on to the spiked railings of the cemetery, and, reaching out with his thin fingers, snatched a yellow rose. He ran in front of Spit and thrust it into a small hole in his jersey.

'I pwesent you with the wose of the winner!' he exclaimed.

'And I've a good mind to present you with a clout on the lug,' replied Spit, 'for pinching a flower from a cemetery. An' what's more, it's bad luck.' Seeing Chick's face, he relented. 'On second thoughts, Chick, I'll wear it. Eee, wot a 'eavenly smell!'

Happily we went along, and Spit turned to a couple of lads at the back. 'Hy, stop that whistling. Don't forget what day it is – folk want their sleep out.'

A faint sweated glow had come over Spit's face when we reached the top of the hill, but he was as majestically calm as ever. Taking the bottle of cold water from his trolley-seat, he put it to his lips and rinsed out his mouth in the manner of a boxer.

The two contestants were called together by Ernie.

'No bumpin' or borin',' he said.

They nodded.

'The winner,' he said, 'is the first who puts the nose of his trolley past the cemetery gates.'

They nodded.

'Now, who,' he asked, 'is to be judge?'

Leslie looked at me. 'I've no objection to Bill,' he said. 'I know he's straight.'

I hadn't realized I was, I thought, but by heck I will be!

'Ernie here,' said Spit, 'can be starter.'

With that Leslie and Spit shook hands.

'Fly down to them gates,' said Ernie to me. He had his father's pigeon-timing watch in his hand. 'I'll be setting 'em off dead on the stroke of ten o'clock.'

I hurried down to the gates. I looked back and saw the supporters lining themselves on either side of the road. Leslie was sitting upright on *The British Queen*. Spit was settling himself to ride belly-down. Ernie Haddock, handkerchief raised in the right hand, eye gazing down on the watch in the left, was counting them off – just like when he tossed one of his father's pigeons.

66

'Five – four – three – two – one – Off!'

Spit was away like a shot. That vigorous toe push sent him clean ahead of Leslie. A volley of shouts went up from his supporters, and groans from Leslie's. I saw Spit move straight to the middle of the road camber. Then I ran ahead to take up my position at the winning-post.

When I turned again I was surprised to see that Spit had not increased the lead. In fact, it seemed that Leslie had begun to gain on him. He had settled himself into a crouched position, and those perfect wheels combined with his extra weight were bringing him up with Spit. Not that it seemed possible he could ever catch him. For Spit, lying flat on his trolley, moving with a fine balance, gliding, as it were, over the rough patches, looked to me as though he were a bird that might suddenly open out its wings and fly clean into the air.

The runners along the side could no longer keep up with the trolleys. And now, as they skimmed past the half-way mark, and came to the very steepest part, there was no doubt that Leslie was gaining. Spit had never ridden better; he coaxed *Egdam* over the tricky parts, swayed with her, gave her her head, and guided her. Yet Leslie, clinging grimly to the steering-rope of *The British Queen*, and riding the rougher part of the road, was actually drawing level. Those beautiful ball-bearing wheels, engineer-made, encased in oil, were holding the road, and bringing Leslie along faster than spirit and skill could carry Spit.

Dead level they sped into the final stretch. Spit's slight figure was poised fearlessly on his trolley, drawing the extremes of speed from her. Thundering beside him, anxious but determined, came Leslie. He was actually drawing ahead – and forcing his way to the top of the camber. On they came like two charioteers – Spit delicately edging to the side, to gain inches by the extra downward momentum. I kept my eyes fastened clean across the road as they came belting past the winning post.

First past the plate was *The British Queen*. I saw that first. Then I saw the heavy rear wheel jog over a pothole and strike Spit's front wheel – sending him in a swerve across the road. Suddenly then, from nowhere, a charabanc came speeding round the wide bend.

Spit was straight in its path. Nothing could avoid the collision. I gave a cry of fear as I saw the heavy solid tyre of the front wheel hit the trolley. Spit was flung up and his back hit the radiator. Then the driver stopped dead.

I got there first. Spit was lying on the macadam road on his side. His face was white and dusty, and coming out between his lips and trickling down his chin was a rivulet of fresh red blood. Scattered all about him were yellow rose petals.

'Not my fault,' I heard the driver shouting. 'I didn't have a chance. He came straight at me.'

The next thing we were surrounded by women who had got out of the charabanc. And then Leslie and all the lads came up.

'Somebody send for an ambulance!' called a woman.

'I'll run an' tell the gatekeeper to telephone,' said Ernie Haddock.

'I hadn't a chance,' the driver explained to the women.

'A piece of his jersey on the starting-handle there . . .' said someone.

'Don't move him,' said the driver to a stout woman who had bent over Spit. 'Wait for the ambulance.'

'Hush up,' she said. She knelt and put a silk scarf under Spit's head. Then she wiped his mouth with her little handkerchief.

He opened his eyes. Glazed they were, as though he couldn't see. A short cough came out of him, then he looked at me and his lips moved.

'Who won?'

'Thee!' blurted out Leslie. 'Tha just licked me. Eh, Bill?'

'Aye,' I said, 'old *Egdam* just pipped *The British Queen.*'

Spit's eyes closed again. The women looked at each other. They nearly all had tears in their eyes. Then Spit looked up again, and his wise, knowing look came over his face. After a minute he spoke in a sharp whisper:

'Liars. I can remember seeing Leslie's back wheel hit my front 'un. I didn't win—I lost.' He stared upward for a few seconds, then his eyes twitched and shut.

The driver kept repeating how it wasn't his fault, and next thing the ambulance came. Nearly all the women were crying now, and I saw the look that went between the two men who put Spit on a stretcher—but I couldn't believe he was dead. I had to go into the ambulance with the attendant to give him particulars. I went up the step and sat down inside and looked out of the little window as the driver slammed the doors. I saw the driver holding Leslie as a witness. Chick Dale was lifting the smashed-up *Egdam* on to the body of *The British Queen*. People with bunches of flowers in their hands stared after us as we drove off. Then I heard the ambulance man asking me Spit's name. Then he touched me on the elbow with his pencil and said:

'Where did he live?'

I knew then. That word 'did' struck right into me. But for a minute I couldn't answer. I had to think hard, for the way he said it made it suddenly seem as though Spit Nolan had been dead and gone for ages.

STEPHEN CORRIN

Federigo's Falcon

from *The Decameron* by Boccaccio

In the beautiful Italian city of Florence there once lived a handsome young man called Federigo who was more famed for his knightly deeds of arms and for his courtesy to gentlewomen than any other man in the city. Now Federigo fell passionately in love with a rich young widow called Giovanna, one of the most beautiful women of her time. In her honour, and to show how much he loved her, Federigo arranged many elaborate tournaments, banquets and entertainments and he also sent her lavish gifts of great cost and rarity. The fair Lady Giovanna did not pay much attention either to them or to the man who was responsible for them, but Federigo was not discouraged, nor did he love her any the less. However, there came a day when he had spent so much of his wealth on these feasts and joustings and presents that he had hardly any money left and found himself deep in debt. He was obliged to sell his fine mansion, his horses and stables, and to go and live on a small farm in the country. One of his possessions, how-ever, he refused to sell: that was his falcon, one of the best in the world, which he loved dearly.

Now it so happened that during the summer season

the Lady Giovanna came to live on her country estate with her young son and that this estate was quite close to Federigo's modest farm. From time to time, when Federigo was out hunting with his beloved falcon, the boy would come and visit Federigo and occasionally he would play with the falcon. In time he became very attached to the clever bird and he told his mother how fond he was of it and how dearly he would like to have it for himself.

'My dear son,' said Lady Giovanna, 'I very much fear that this will not be possible. Federigo was once a very wealthy man but now he is poor and the falcon is the only precious thing that he owns. You must be content with watching and playing with it from time to time when Federigo permits you.' The lad had no choice but to accept his mother's sensible words on the matter.

A few months later the boy fell gravely ill. The doctors, even the most learned and famous, tried everything they knew to help him to get well, but their efforts were all in vain. The boy just lay in his bed, deathly pale, eating hardly anything and barely speaking. The poor Lady Giovanna was at her wits' end. She would gladly have given her own life to make her son well again. But his condition grew worse and worse and finally the doctors gave up hope.

Very early one morning, pale and worn after sitting by his bedside all night, Giovanna bent over her son and whispered, almost deliriously, 'My poor, poor boy,

72

please, please get well for my sake. You are all I have in the world. What can I get for you to make you strong again? I promise I will get you anything in the world you could wish to have.' The sick lad stirred in his bed and muttered, 'Mother . . . Federigo's falcon . . . I think . . . if I could have that falcon I could get well very quickly.'

Lady Giovanna sprang up. She knew all about that famous falcon, how dearly Federigo loved it and how much her son had become attached to it. She knew too how much Federigo had loved her in the past and how he had spent nearly all his riches trying to win her favour and she had never given him the slightest hope or encouragement. 'How can I be so ungenerous?' she asked herself, 'as to ask him now to part with the one thing which he loves best in the world?' But one quick glance at her son's wan face dispelled all hesitation and doubt from her mind. 'Yes, dear boy,' she whispered, leaning over to him again, 'I shall go to Federigo to-morrow morning and bring back his falcon to you.' The boy gave a faint smile and sank into a light sleep.

Next morning she set out for Federigo's little farm-house, accompanied by her maid. She found Federigo working in his garden. He was overjoyed to see Giovanna. 'You do me a great honour, dear lady, to visit my house. You are most welcome, you and your friend.' But in his heart he could not help feeling sur-prised at this most unexpected call from a woman he loved so dearly.

Lady Giovanna said: 'Please excuse me for calling

upon you like this, without warning. I know I have treated you ungraciously in the past and I should like to make amends in some small way.' She hesitated, then she said, 'May I and my companion share luncheon with you today?'

'My dear lady,' said Federigo warmly, 'I am not aware that you have ever treated me other than with the greatest kindness. My wealth, as you know, is all spent, but I would gladly spend it all over again just for the joy of having your company at lunch.'

He then led them into the house and asked them to make themselves at home while he prepared the meal.

He ran into his kitchen, only to find that the cupboards were almost bare. Neither was there any food stored in the larder. Federigo was in despair. How he wished for those past days when he had been in a position to give so many banquets in Lady Giovanna's honour! It was getting late. He must not keep the ladies waiting. Suddenly his eyes fell upon his handsome falcon sitting on its perch in a tiny room adjoining the kitchen. 'That bird would make a dish fit for any lady,' he thought sadly and then, without further ado, choking back his tears, he seized it and wrung its neck. He called the farmer's daughter from next door and asked her to pluck it and roast it on the spit ready for the meal. Then he laid the table with an exquisite white linen cloth and went and told the ladies that a modest meal had been prepared and was awaiting their pleasure.

And so all three sat down to their meal, at which

Federigo played the host with great charm and dignity. Neither Lady Giovanna, nor, of course, her companion, had the faintest suspicion of what kind of bird it was they were enjoying.

When the meal was over and Lady Giovanna had thanked Federigo for his gracious hospitality, they went and sat in the garden and chatted.

'After all your kindness,' said Giovanna, 'you may be surprised that I have the audacity to ask you a further favour. But I imagine you must have realized by now that I have come here for a special purpose.' Federigo looked at her beautiful face in expectant surprise.

'You know I have a son who is to me the most precious thing in the world. You know him well, for he has been here often and has frequently gone hawking with you. He is very fond of you and admires you very much. At this moment he is gravely ill and there is nothing the doctors can do for him. But there is one thing that might possibly help him and as a mother I have a duty to get it for him. I am speaking of your beautiful falcon. I feel a deep shame in asking this, but if you can save my son's life by giving it to him, I shall never, ever, forget you.'

At these words Federigo sat for a moment speechless with dismay and astonishment.

At last he said: 'Dear Lady Giovanna, what you have just told me has made me the saddest man on this earth. There is nothing in the world I would not do for you or your son and yet this one seemingly simple thing I cannot do.' Lady Giovanna rose as if to leave, saying, 'I understand . . . I really had no right . . .' but Federigo quickly interrupted her. 'Please be seated, dear lady. Let me explain.' And, his voice trembling slightly, he continued: 'When you did me the great honour of coming to share a meal with me I was in despair, for my larder contained nothing worthy of you. Then I thought of my falcon. He has grown nice and fat, I thought, and should make a tasty dish. In that respect, at least, I hope you were not disappointed' (he added these last words with a bitter smile). He then had the farmer's daughter bring in the pathetic remnants of the beautiful bird.

Lady Giovanna exclaimed, 'How could you find it in you to kill such a magnificent bird, a bird to which you and my poor son were so passionately attached!' But inwardly she thought, 'How magnificently noble of this man! And how generous! And how deep must be his feelings for me. How can I ever forget this brave gesture or repay him for it!' Then with great sadness she said goodbye to Federigo and thanked him for the honour he had shown her.

Returning home to her son empty-handed, she hardly had the strength to tell him of the failure of her mission. She mumbled some feeble excuse about a certain delay before the falcon would arrive, but there was such a lack of conviction in her words that the poor lad had no difficulty in guessing the real truth of the matter. Two days later he died.

After several months of inconsolable grief she found herself alone with a large estate to manage, and all her friends kept persuading her to remarry. She at first dismissed the idea with ridicule but finally she said, as though this would put them off the idea, 'Well, dear friends, if I must marry again it will be to Federigo, for there is no finer man on earth.' Her friends were amazed. 'Why,' they exclaimed, 'that poor fellow has not a penny to bless himself with. You will be marrying a noble beggar.'

'I know that only too well,' she replied feelingly. 'But I would rather marry a man without money than mere money without a true man. It is Federigo or nobody!'

A few weeks later Giovanna and Federigo were married. They found comfort and joy in one another and lived for many years in peace and happiness.

Daedalus and Icarus

The sun ruled the sky above the island. The sea licked about its shores, catching the light and glittering. The land absorbed the brightness of the sun, but the sun and sea seemed to talk together.

The sea was the Aegean, of gods and heroes, the island Crete.

To Crete across the sea there fled a man called Daedalus. He was an engineer, the most brilliant inventor of his time and no one more aware of that than he. Indeed his pride had led to this present flight; for when the skill of his nephew Talos had come near to rivalling his own, jealous Daedalus had pushed him from a rooftop to his death and, as punishment, had been exiled from Athens, city of his birth. He took with him into exile his young son Icarus. He idolized this boy. To hear him talk, you might think he'd invented him, not merely fathered him.

On Crete at Cnossus stood a palace, brilliant in the sun. Striped pillars supported it, and no one could have counted all its chambers, courts and halls. In the greatest of them sat Minos, King of Crete, on a throne inlaid with gold. He was mighty, a sun among other kings, ruling an empire of subject states all round the Aegean Sea. Before him even proud Daedalus came bowing low.

'Welcome, Daedalus, welcome to our court, O subtle engineer! Your name is known to us; we have heard also of your skill, which makes you doubly welcome here: for we have a task to meet such skill as yours. Indeed its accomplishment is the price of our hospitality to yourself and to your son.'

Minos rose from his throne, led Daedalus and Icarus to a door set with iron bars. From the room beyond came a warmth, a stench like a farmyard.

'We desire you to build us a stronghold beneath our house from which nothing, from which no one, can escape, neither man nor monster, not even monsters so mighty, so awful as this; for see, O Daedalus, our son, the Minotaur.'

Its hands that came to grasp the bars were huge but human hands with hair upon them curled and black, each hair as thick, as stiff as wire. Its limbs were human shaped, though hard as wood.

It glared at Daedalus with red, small, furious eyes, then opened its cavernous red mouth and roared at him, flinging back its head, the bludgeon head of a huge black bull.

Daedalus bowed to the king again.

'Great king, you are great indeed, but you could choose no better architect than I. The prison I construct will make the names of Minos and of Daedalus remembered for the rest of time. And I swear by Apollo, by Hephaestus the craftsmen's god, that no man, no monster, could escape from it.'

Daedalus drew plans first, scratching them out on tablets of yellow wax, plans too complex for any to decipher but himself. Then he set troops of slaves and labourers to work, enough men to make an army. Deep beneath the palace with picks and spades and hammers, they gouged out the rocks of Crete. Some hacked and smashed at them till the sparks flew off. Some carried the rubble away in baskets on their backs; yet others cut props and pillars to support the roof.

Little by little they tunnelled from the bitter rock a labyrinth, a maze, an intricate confusion of tunnels and passages, with so many false turnings and alleyways that a hundred men could have wandered there or a hundred rivers flowed and neither man nor river ever met another.

In the labyrinth then lived the Minotaur, its roar confined in rock still heard dimly through the palace. People trembled hearing it. Minos, they knew, sent those who had angered him to feed his son, and to the Minotaur all alike were men of tender flesh to tear and devour – Cretan, Spartan, Athenian, none could withstand its furious charge from some dark winding of the labyrinth.

Daedalus, meanwhile, lived on at Cnossus in the service of the king. He seemed to grow more clever, more ingenious than ever. He copied in iron a fish's backbone with its row of little teeth; this made the first saw ever seen. He fitted together two pointed rods of iron to make compasses with which a perfect circle could be drawn. His fame grew, all over Greece, all round the Aegean Sea. His pride also burned and puffed itself up till he thought his skill equal to a god's. The sun of Minos' favour shone on him more brilliantly each day, and nothing seemed likely to move him from the favour of the king.

But then one day guards came to seize Daedalus and Icarus and drag them before Minos the king. And he was wrathful, furious, bellowing like a bull himself, like his son the Minotaur.

'So you boasted, Daedalus, that no one could escape your labyrinth. But the Minotaur is dead. A man has killed our son and understood the maze and sailed away unharmed from Crete. Now you and your son shall be cast into the maze, and if you too escape from there, you'll get no further, we swear to it. We, Minos, do not swear in vain. We rule not merely Crete but all the sea about. Without ships no man can escape from Crete, and you, O subtle architect, clever as you are, you command no ships upon our Aegean Sea.'

So Daedalus, with Icarus his son, was cast into the prison he had made. He took with him there a ball of golden thread, which looked in such darkness like an image of the golden sun. This was the device he'd made secretly to guide himself to the far end of the labyrinth. He tied one end to the entrance place, and slowly the ball began to unroll ahead of them, through all the turns and windings, the confusions of entrances and alleyways. After a while Daedalus smelt a familiar, farmyard reek, but it had a fouler, sicklier note to it, and the stench went on growing all the time till they reached the cave at the heart of the labyrinth where the corpse of the Minotaur lay rotting on dirty straw.

It seemed feeble now, and foolish and puny. Its red eyes were closed, its limbs flaccid and limp. Only the yellow horns still looked dangerous. Daedalus gazed beyond it, shuddering, holding up his little lamp till its light reached the farthest corners of the cave, where human bones and skulls lay scattered everywhere. There were feathers also from birds devoured by the Minotaur. He picked up one and examined minutely its shaft and quill.

'Minos rules the land of Crete,' he said. 'He may rule the sea that surrounds it too. But remember, Icarus my son, remember that great King Minos does not rule the sky.'

Icarus did not know what his father meant by this. He watched Daedalus lay feathers overlapping in four separate rows, each diminishing in size from one end to the other. Then Daedalus brought from his tunic a cake of wax, a needle, and some fine strong thread. He joined the larger feathers with the needle and thread. He softened the wax in the warmth of the lamp and used it to unite the smaller feathers.

Icarus watched his father's patient hands, watched

small feathers waver in the heat above the lamp and the wax drip down in slow, dull drops. Sometimes Daedalus made him hold feathers or pull on an end of thread, and he was eager to help, too eager perhaps, jogging his father's arm or letting his shadow fall across the light.

At last Daedalus took the completed rows, bent them and curved them into shape, and then his son could see what they were meant to be; how from the wings of birds, his father Daedalus had made wings for men, one pair each for himself and Icarus.

The oil of the lamp was all burned by now. As they left the cave the wick flickered and went out so that their only light was in the guiding thread, in the diminishing golden ball, which unrolled ahead of them towards the secret entrance of the labyrinth where no guards would stand in wait. The sound of their breathing magnified itself. On and on they went. Even when they neared the end, there was still no light, not the narrowest rim or chink. The thread doubled round and back again, and they twisted confusedly to follow it.

The light broke suddenly, burst upon them. They had to bury their eyes against the blinding, burning sun. The air rushed at them too, strong air full of honey and wild thyme, for this entrance to the labyrinth lay on the hillside by Cnossus, within sight of the glittering sea.

When Daedalus' eyes accepted light at last, he took some leather thongs and fixed the smaller pair of wings to the arms of Icarus. He fixed the larger to his own, explaining all the while what they had to do. They would have to use their arms just as the wing bones of a bird, making the feathers gently rise and fall.

'But mind, mind, Icarus, my son, don't fly too low, too near the sea, for the feathers once wet will not carry you. But then do not fly too high, too near the sun, for the sun's heat, like the lamp's, will melt the wax, make the feathers fall away.'

Icarus heard his father out. But he was already impatient to begin, moving his arms experimentally, so that the air caught the feathers on the wings.

Daedalus started to run along the hillside. When he had gained some speed he jumped into the air, shouting at Icarus to follow him. Both moved their arms with awkward, chopping strokes; they did not soar as they had expected to, but struggled jerkily, not far above the rock. Daedalus kept close to Icarus, instructing him, but made no more elegant a bird himself. If an even stroke did make him soar, he would lose the knack at once and slip down again. Once Icarus, shooting up, met Daedalus struggling down, their wings entangled and both fell hard on to the bruising stone.

Icarus caught it first, the rhythm, the pattern of flight. He swept into the air and away, filled with joyfulness, shouting with delight, and almost at once Daedalus followed his son up into the sky. Their arms flowed so smoothly up and down, the feathers took on such life and force, that they did not seem like arms

any more, the bones felt fluid, supple, the slighter bones of wings. The air felt different, too, solid, protective, strong – it held, filled, surrounded them, while above stood the golden beaming sun.

Higher and higher flew Daedalus and Icarus. Down below on land men began to notice them. Farmers leaned on their ploughs and looked up into the sky, shading their eyes against the sun. Washerwomen dropped the clothes they scrubbed, fishermen let fall their nets, boat-builders laid down the saws that Daedalus had made. When they began to fly across the sea, sailors came running to the sides of ships to stare at them. All imagined they saw gods not men.

Daedalus felt like a god. He was the inventor of human flight, the first mortal man to fly. He shouted to the air, the sun, the sea, exultantly.

'What say you mighty gods? You have changed men into birds to make them fly. Icarus remains a boy yet flies like an eagle through the air.'

Icarus flew more like a gull than an eagle now, skimming low, delightfully, across the shimmer of sea so that his father had to shout and wave to him to keep the feathers dry. Though annoyed at first to be taken from his game he was soon seized by still greater joy, moving his arms in more and more powerful strokes, swooping, soaring upwards in the sky like the eagle his father imagined him.

Daedalus returned to his godlike dreams and failed to watch the flight of Icarus.

'Other men need gods to make them fly. Icarus has only his mortal father Daedalus.'

Higher and higher flew Icarus, towards the strengthening sun. The air grew hotter, the sun more brilliant, dazzling to his eyes. He had forgotten all warnings now, flying nearer as if drawn to it, like a moth towards a lamp.

And slowly the wax on his wings began to melt. It softened gently, then dripped a little, in slow, thick drops. A feather slipped from it, fell drifting, turning, down towards the sea. Other feathers followed, singly at first, but then more and more of them at once. And suddenly, though the ecstatic Icarus as confidently moved his wings, there were not enough feathers left to hold the air, to keep him up in flight.

His father looked back, to see his son plunge headlong, faster than the feathers, passing every one. Straight as a gull he fell towards the sea, but did not swerve in safety like a gull above the glittering waves. He plunged right into the heart of them, and their startled waters closed above his head. All that remained of Icarus were some feathers floating on the sea, while his father flew, weeping, in the sky, alone.

AMBROSE BIERCE

The Man and the Snake

(*In an ancient volume called* The Marvells of Science *Harker Brayton has been reading that the serpent's eye has a magnetic quality which draws people towards it against their will. The serpent then administers the lethal bite.*)

A train of reflections followed – for Brayton was a man of thought – and he unconsciously lowered his book without altering the direction of his eyes. As soon as the volume had gone below the line of sight, something in an obscure corner of the room recalled his attention to his surroundings. What he saw, in the shadow under his bed, were two small points of light, apparently about an inch apart. They might have been reflections of the gas jet above him, in the metal nail heads: he gave them but little thought and resumed his reading. A moment later something – some impulse which it did not occur to him to analyse – impelled him to lower the book again and seek for what he saw before. The points of light were still there. They seemed to have become brighter than before, shining with a greenish lustre which he had not at first observed. He thought, too, that they might have moved a trifle – were somewhat nearer. They were still too much in shadow, however, to reveal their nature and origin to an indolent attention, and he resumed his reading. Suddenly something in the text suggested a thought which made him start and drop the book for the third time to the side of the sofa, whence, escaping from his hand, it fell sprawling to the floor, back upward. Brayton, half risen, was staring intently into the obscurity beneath the bed, where the points of light shone with, it seemed to him, an added fire. His attention was now fully aroused, his gaze eager and imperative. It disclosed, almost directly beneath the foot-rail beneath the bed, the coils of a large serpent – the points of light were its eyes! Its horrible head, thrust flatly forth from the innermost coil and resting upon the outermost, was directed towards him, the definition of the wide, brutal jaw and the idiot-like forehead serving to show the direction of its malevolent gaze. The eyes were no longer merely luminous points; they looked into his own with a meaning, a malign significance.

A snake in the bedroom of a modern city dwelling of the better sort is, happily, not so common a phenomenon as to make explanations altogether needless. Harker Brayton, a bachelor of thirty-five, a scholar, idler and something of an athlete, had returned to San Francisco from all manner of remote and unfamiliar countries. His tastes being a trifle luxurious, and the resources of the Castle hotel being inadequate, he had gladly accepted the hospitality of his friend, Dr Druring, the distinguished scientist. Dr Druring's house, a large, old-fashioned one in what was now an obscure quarter of the city, had an outer and visible aspect of proud reserve. It had one wing which was a combination of laboratory, menagerie and museum. It was here that the doctor indulged the scientific side of his nature in the study of such forms of animal life as engaged his interest and comforted his taste. His scientific sympathies were distinctly reptilian. His wife and daughters were excluded from what he called the Snakery, which, architecturally, and in point of furnishing, had a severe simplicity befitting the humble simplicity of its occupants, many of whom, indeed, could not safely have been entrusted with the liberty which is necessary to the full enjoyment of luxury; for they had the troublesome peculiarity of being alive. In their own apartments, however, they were under as little personal restraint as was compatible with their protection from the baneful habit of swallowing one another. Despite the Snakery and its uncanny associations – to which, indeed, he gave little attention – Brayton found life at the Druring mansion very much to his mind.

Beyond the smart shock of surprise and a shudder of mere loathing, Mr Brayton was not greatly affected. His first thought was to ring the call-bell and bring a servant; but, although the bell-cord dangled within easy reach, he made no movement towards it; it occurred to his mind that the act might subject him to the suspicion of fear, which he certainly did not feel. He was more keenly conscious of the incongruous nature of the situation than affected by its perils; it was revolting, but absurd.

The reptile was of a species with which Brayton was unfamiliar. Its length he could only conjecture; the body at the largest visible part seemed about as thick as his forearm. In what way was it dangerous, if in any way? Was it venomous? Was it a constrictor? His knowledge of nature's danger signals did not enable him to say; he had never deciphered the code.

If not dangerous, the creature was at least offensive. It was *de trop* – 'matter out of place' – an impertinence. The gem was unworthy of the setting. Even the barbarous taste of our time and country, which had loaded the walls of the room with pictures, the floor with furniture and the furniture with bric-à-brac, had not quite fitted the place for this bit of the savage life of the jungle. Besides – insupportable thought! – the exhalations of its breath mingled with the atmosphere which he himself was breathing!

These thoughts shaped themselves with greater or less definition in Brayton's mind, and begot action. The process is what we call consideration and decision.

Brayton rose to his feet and prepared to back softly away from the snake, without disturbing it, if possible, and through the door. People retire so from the presence of the great, for greatness is power, and power is a menace. He knew that he could walk backward without obstruction, and find the door without error. Should the monster follow, the taste which had plastered the walls with paintings had consistently supplied a rack of murderous Oriental weapons from which he could snatch one to suit the occasion. In the meantime the snake's eyes burned with a more pitiless malevolence than ever.

Brayton lifted his right foot free of the floor to step backward. That moment he felt a strong aversion to doing so.

'I am accounted brave,' he murmured; 'is bravery, then, no more than pride? Because there are none to witness the shame shall I retreat?'

He was steadying himself with his right hand upon the back of a chair, his foot suspended.

'Nonsense!' he said aloud; 'I am not so great a coward as to fear to seem to myself afraid.'

He lifted the foot a little higher by slightly bending the knee, and thrust it sharply to the floor – an inch in front of the other! He could not think how that occurred. A trial with the left foot had the same result; it was again in advance of the right. The hand upon the chair-back was grasping it; the arm was straight, reaching somewhat backward. One might have seen that he was reluctant to lose his hold. The snake's malignant head was still thrust forth from the inner coil as before, the neck level. It had not moved, but its eyes were now electric sparks, radiating an infinity of luminous needles.

The man had an ashy pallor. Again he took a step forward, and another, partly dragging the chair, which, when finally released, fell upon the floor with a crash. The man groaned; the snake made neither sound nor motion, but its eyes were two dazzling suns. The reptile itself was wholly concealed by them. They gave off enlarging rings of rich and vivid colours, which at their greatest expansion successively vanished like soap bubbles; they seemed to approach his very face, and anon were an immeasurable distance away. He heard, somewhere, the continuous throbbing of a great drum, with desultory bursts of far music, inconceivably sweet, like the tones of an Aeolian harp. He knew it for the sunrise melody of Memnon's statue, and thought he stood in the Nileside reeds, hearing, with exalted sense, that immortal anthem through the silence of the centuries.

The music ceased; rather, it became by insensible degrees the distant roll of a retreating thunderstorm. A landscape, glittering with sun and rain, stretched before him, arched with a vivid rainbow, framing in its giant curve a hundred visible cities. In the middle distance a vast serpent, wearing a crown, reared its head out of its voluminous convolutions and looked at him with his dead mother's eyes. Suddenly this enchanting landscape seemed to rise swiftly upward, like a drop-scene at a theatre, and vanished in a blank. Something struck him a hard blow upon the face and breast. He had fallen to the floor; the blood ran from his broken nose and his bruised lips. For a moment he was dazed and stunned, and lay with closed eyes, his face against the floor. In a few moments he had recovered, and then realized that his fall, by withdrawing his eyes, had broken the spell which held him. He felt that now, by keeping his gaze averted, he would be able to retreat. But the thought of the serpent within a few feet of his head, yet unseen — perhaps in the very act of springing upon him and throwing its coils about his throat — was too horrible. He lifted his head, stared again into those baleful eyes, and was again in bondage.

The snake had not moved, and appeared somewhat to have lost its power upon the imagination; the gorgeous illusions of a few moments before were not repeated. Beneath that flat and brainless brow its black, beady eyes simply glittered, as at first, with an expression unspeakably malignant. It was as if the creature, knowing its triumph assured, had determined to practise no more alluring wiles.

Now ensued a fearful scene. The man, prone upon the floor, within a yard of his enemy, raised the upper part of his body upon his elbows, his head thrown back, his legs extended to their full length. His face was white between its gouts of blood; his eyes were strained open to their uttermost expansion. There was froth upon his lips; it dropped off in flakes. Strong convulsions ran through his body, making almost serpentine undulations. He bent himself at the waist, shifting his legs from side to side. And every movement left him a little

nearer to the snake. He thrust his hand forward to brace himself back, yet constantly advanced upon his elbows.

Dr Druring and his wife sat in the library. The scientist was in rare good humour.

'I have just obtained, by exchange with another collector,' he said, 'a splendid specimen of the ophiophagus.'

'And what may that be?' the lady inquired with a somewhat languid interest.

'Why bless my soul, what profound ignorance! My dear, a man who ascertains after marriage that his wife does not know Greek, is entitled to a divorce. The ophiophagus is a snake which eats other snakes.'

'I hope it will eat all yours,' she said, absently shifting the lamp. 'But how does it get the other snakes? By charming them, I suppose.'

'That is just like you, dear,' said the doctor, with an affectation of petulance. 'You know how irritating to me is any allusion to that vulgar superstition about the snake's power of fascination.'

The conversation was interrupted by a mighty cry, which rang through the silent house like the voice of a demon shouting in a tomb! Again and yet again it sounded, with terrible distinctness. They sprang to their feet, the man confused, the lady pale and speechless with fright. Almost before the echoes of the last cry had died away, the doctor was out of the room, springing up the staircase two steps at a time. In the corridor, in front of Brayton's chamber, he met some servants who had come from the upper floor. Together they rushed at the door without knocking. It was unfastened and gave way. Brayton lay upon his stomach on the floor, dead. His head and arms were partly concealed under the foot-rail of the bed. They pulled the body away, turning it upon the back. The face was daubed with blood and froth, the eyes were wide open, staring – a dreadful sight!

'Died in a fit,' said the scientist, bending his knee and placing his hand upon the heart. While in that position, he happened to glance under the bed. 'Good God!' he added, 'how did this thing get in here?'

He reached under the bed, pulled out the snake, and flung it, still coiled, to the centre of the room, whence, with a harsh, shuffling sound, it slid across the polished floor till stopped by the wall, where it lay without motion. It was a stuffed snake; its eyes were two shoe buttons.

Lady Godiva

The city of Coventry is one of our greatest industrial towns, famous for its production of cars, motor cycles and aeroplanes, and also for its splendid new cathedral. Nine hundred years ago it was even more important, for it was the fourth largest city in England; only London, Bristol and York were bigger. It was ruled by a very powerful man called Leofric, who lived in a magnificent castle with a huge retinue of guards and serving people of all kinds. Even in those days Coventry was a very busy centre, making leather and woollen goods and soap. But most of its inhabitants were distressingly poor and Leofric forced them to pay heavy taxes so that he could live in luxury in his castle. His wife, Lady Godiva, was very unhappy about this, but there was nothing she could do.

One day, at the end of a month when Leofric had spent more than his usual quota on horses, wine and meats, he decided to levy a further tax upon the long-suffering inhabitants of Coventry. When this terrible news came to the ears of the people they gathered in great crowds outside his castle to beg their lord not to impose this further heavy burden upon them. Lady

Godiva, watching from a high window, could see the women and children dressed in rags, pale and underfed, and the men gaunt and sunken-eyed. She could see the guards down below driving the people brutally away and she realized that her husband did not care one whit about what happened to the ordinary people of Coventry.

She hurried down to her husband and burst into the room where he was consulting with one of his stewards.

'. . . and see to it that this tax is collected promptly,' Leofric was saying. He turned angrily to Godiva. 'And pray what is the meaning of this, wife? You know I am not to be disturbed when I am discussing important financial affairs with Godfrey here.'

'I must speak with you, my lord,' said Lady Godiva.

Leofric looked at his beautiful wife and relented slightly. 'What is it?' he asked.

'I have been watching those wretched, miserable, starving people from my window and I know that it will be impossible for them to raise this new tax.' Her big blue eyes were moist with pity.

Leofric stared at her, then smiled. 'Pray return to your tapestry, good wife,' he said. 'These matters do not concern a woman.'

'But they *are* my concern,' persisted Lady Godiva. 'These ill-fed, ragged people are my fellow-citizens and I cannot help being touched by their wretched plight.'

'Enough, enough,' said Leofric. 'I am busy. Please leave us.'

Lady Godiva went down on her knees. 'My dear lord and husband,' she said, 'I will do anything you ask if you release the people from this burdensome tax.'

Leofric was looking down absent-mindedly at the documents spread out before him on the table, but at the word 'anything' he turned round sharply.

'Did you say "anything"?' he asked.

'Yes, my lord, anything.'

'Well,' he said, 'if you ride naked through the streets of Coventry, I will not only repeal this tax but will also give you three bags of gold to distribute to the poor.'

Lady Godiva looked startled and her eyes filled with tears. She rose from her knees and hurried to the door. Then she turned round and looked Leofric straight in the eye.

'Very well, my lord,' she said quietly and deliberately, and left the room.

Then she went to her room, and penned the following letter:

My Dear Unhappy People of Coventry,

I know well how grieved you all are by the news of the new tax which my lord and husband has levied upon you. I am now able to tell you that the tax will be repealed provided I will ride naked through the streets of our city. For your sake I have told my lord and husband that I am prepared to do this. I have made this painful decision because I have confidence that you, citizens of Coventry, will respect my modesty.

I therefore ask you, dear kind people, to remain indoors tomorrow morning between the hours of ten and twelve o'clock and to keep your shutters closed.

She then signed the letter simply 'Godiva' and dispatched it with a herald, ordering him to see that every man, woman and child became aware of its contents.

The next morning she ordered her white mare to be brought to the castle gates at ten o'clock. Alone in her chamber she removed the hair pins from her magnificently long, flaxen tresses. Then she undressed, and her beautiful hair fell loosely over her shoulders and hung down to cover most of her body. She went to the gates, mounted her white steed and set off through the streets of Coventry. There was an eerie stillness over the city. Every person was indoors and all the shutters were drawn. Did I say 'all'? Well, except for one house, where a tailor called Tom could not conquer his curiosity and had drawn his shutter slightly aside so that he might see the gallant lady. (Later this tailor became known to all the world as 'Peeping Tom' and there is even a legend which says that he was immediately struck with blindness as a punishment for his inquisitiveness.)

Lady Godiva rode calmly through the city and arrived back at her castle just as the church bells rang for mid-day.

Lord Leofric was so full of admiration for his wife's bravery and generosity that he not only kept his word –

repealing the tax and giving her three bags of gold for the poor – but from that day onwards made up his mind to treat his citizens less harshly.

As for Lady Godiva, she is remembered by the people of Coventry to this very day and every year her courageous action on their behalf is celebrated with much pomp and pageantry. And in one of Coventry's old houses you can see the figure of a man peeping through one of the windows.

A Sailor's Yarn

'Once upon a time there was a clipper ship called the *Mary*, and she was lying in Panama waiting for a freight. It was hot, and it was calm, and it was hazy, and the men aboard her were dead sick of the sight of her. They had been lying there all the summer, having nothing to do but to wash her down and scrape the royal masts with glass, and make the chain cables bright. And aboard of her was a big A.B. from Liverpool, with a tattooed chest on him and an arm like a spar. And this man's name was Bill.

'Now, one day, while the captain of this clipper was sunning in the club, there came a merchant to him offering him a fine freight home and "despatch" in loading. So the old man went aboard that very evening in a merry temper, and bade the mates rastle the hands aft. He told them that they could go ashore the next morning for a "liberty-day" of four-and-twenty hours, with twenty dollars' pay to blue, and no questions asked if they came aboard drunk. So forward goes all hands merrily, to rout out their go-ashore things, their red handkerchiefs, and "sombre-airers", for to astonish the Dons. And ashore they goes the next morning, after breakfast, with their silver dollars in their fists, and the jolly-boat to take them. And ashore they steps, and "So long" they says to the young fellows in the boat, and so up the Mole to the beautiful town of Panama.

'Now the next morning that fellow Bill I told you of was tacking down the city to the boat, singing some song or another. And when he got near to the jetty he went fumbling in his pocket for his pipe, and what should he find but a silver dollar that had slipped away and been saved. So he thinks, "If I go aboard with this dollar, why the hands'll laugh at me; besides, it's a wasting of it not to spend it." So he casts about for some place where he could blue it in.

'Now close by where he stood there was a sort of a great store, kept by a Johnny Dago. And if I were to tell you of the things they had in it, I would need nine tongues and an oiled hinge to each of them. But Billy walked into this store, into the space inside, into like the 'tween decks, for to have a look about him before buying. And there were great bunches of bananas a-ripening against the wall. And sacks of dried raisins, and bags of dried figs, and melon seeds, and pomegranates enough to sink you. Then there were cotton bales, and calico, and silk of Persia. And rum in puncheons, and bottled ale. And all manner of sweets, and a power of a lot of chemicals. And anchors gone rusty, fished up from the bay after the ships were gone. And spare cables, all ranged for letting go. And ropes, and sails, and balls of marline stuff. Then there were blocks of all kinds, wood and iron. Dunnage there was, and scantling, likewise sea-chests with pictures on them. And casks of beef and pork, and paint, and peas, and petroleum. But for not one of these things did Billy care a handful of bilge.

'Then there were medical comforts, such as ginger and calavances. And plug tobacco, and coil tobacco, and tobacco leaf, and tobacco clippings. And such a power of a lot of bulls' hides as you never saw. Likewise there was tinned things like cocoa, and boxed things like China tea. And any quantity of blankets, and rugs, and donkeys' breakfasts. And oilskins there was, and rubber sea-boots, shore-shoes, and Crimee shirts. Also dungarees, and soap, and matches, so many as you never heard tell. But no, not for one of these things was Bill going for to bargain.

'Then there were lamps and candles, and knives and nutmeg-graters. and things made of bright tin and saucers of red clay; and rolls of coloured cloth, made in the hills by the Indians. Bowls there were painted with twisty-twirls by the folk of old time. And flutes from the tombs (of the Incas), and whistles that looked like flower-pots. Also fiddles and beautiful melodeons. Then there were paper roses for ornament, and false white flowers for graves; also paint-brushes and coir-brooms. There were cages full of parrots, both green and grey; and white cockatoos on perches a-nodding their red crests; and Java love-birds a-billing, and parrakeets a-screaming, and little kittens for the ship with rats. And at the last of all there was a little monkey, chained to a sack of jib-hanks, who sat upon his tail a-grinning.

'Now Bill he sees this monkey, and he thinks he never see a cuter little beast, not never. And then he thinks of something, and he pipes up to the old Johnny Dago, and he says, pointing to the monkey:

'"Hey-a Jonny! How much-a-take-a little munk?"

'So the old Johnny Dago looks at Bill a spell, and then says:

'"I take-a five-a doll' that-a little munk."

'So Bill planks down his silver dollar, and says:

'"I give-a one doll', you cross-eyed Dago."

'Then the old man unchained the monkey, and handed him to Bill, without another word. And away the pair of them went, down the Mole to where the boats lay, where a lanchero took them off to the *Mary*.

'Now when they got aboard all hands came around Bill, saying: "Why, Bill, whatever are you going to do with that there little monkey?" And Bill he said: "You shut your heads about that there little monkey. I'm going to teach that little monkey how to speak. And when he can speak I'm going to sell him to a museum. And then I'll buy a farm. I won't come to sea any more." So they just laugh at Bill, and by and by the *Mary* loaded, and got her hatches on, and sailed south-away, on the road home to Liverpool.

'Well, every evening in the dog-watch, after supper, while the decks were drying from the washing-down, Bill used to take the monkey on the fo'c's'le head, and

set him on the capstan. "Well, ye little divvle," he used to say, "will ye speak? Are ye going to speak, hey?" and the monkey would just grin and chatter back at Billy, but never no Christian speech came in front of them teeth of his. And this game went on until they were up with the Horn, in bitter cold weather, running east like a stag, with a great sea piling up astern. And then one night, at eight bells, Billy came on deck for the first watch, bringing the monkey with him. It was blowing like sin, stiff and cold, and the *Mary* was butting through, and dipping her fo'c's'le under. So Bill takes the monkey, and lashes him down good and snug on the drum of the capstan, on the fo'c's'le head. "Now, ye little divvle," he said, "will ye speak? Will ye speak, eh?" But the monkey just grinned at him.

'At the end of the first hour he came again. "Are ye going to speak, ye little beggar?" he says and the monkey sits and shivers, but never a word does the little beggar say. And it was the same at four bells, when the lookout man was relieved. But at six bells Billy came again, and the monkey looked mighty cold, and it was a wet perch where he was roosting, and his teeth chattered; yet he didn't speak, not so much as a cat. So just before eight bells, when the watch was nearly out, Billy went forward for the last time. "If he don't speak now," says Billy, "overboard he goes for a dumb animal."

'Well, the cold green seas had pretty nearly drowned that little monkey, and the spray had frozen him over like a jacket of ice, and right blue his lips were, and an

icicle was a-dangling from his chin, and he was shiver-
ing like he had an ague. "Well, ye little divvle," says
Billy, "for the last time, will ye speak? Are ye going to
speak, hey?" And the monkey spoke. "*Speak* is it? *Speak*
is it?" he says. "It's so cold it's enough to make a little
fellow *swear*."

'It's the solemn gospel truth that story is.'

Nine Needles

One of the more spectacular minor happenings of the past few years which I am sorry that I missed took place in Columbus, Ohio, home of some friends of a friend of mine. It seems that a Mr Albatross, while looking for something in his medicine cabinet one morning, discovered a bottle of a kind of patent medicine which his wife had been taking for a stomach ailment. Now, Mr Albatross is one of those apprehensive men who are afraid of patent medicines and almost everything else. Some weeks before, he had encountered a paragraph in a Consumers' Research bulletin which announced that this particular medicine was bad for you. He had thereupon ordered his wife to throw out what was left of her supply of the stuff and never buy any more. She had promised, and here now was another bottle of the perilous liquid. Mr Albatross, a man given to quick rages, shouted the conclusion of the story at my friend: 'I threw the bottle out of the bathroom window and the medicine chest after it!' It seems to me that must have been a spectacle worth going a long way to see.

I am sure that many a husband has wanted to wrench

the family medicine cabinet off the wall and throw it out of the window, if only because the average medicine cabinet is so filled with mysterious bottles and unidentifiable objects of all kinds that it is a source of constant bewilderment and exasperation to the American male. Surely the British medicine cabinet, and the French medicine cabinet and all the other medicine cabinets must be simpler and better ordered than ours. It may be that the American habit of saving everything and never throwing anything away, even empty bottles, causes the domestic cabinet to become as cluttered in its small way as the American attic becomes cluttered in its major way. I have encountered few medicine cabinets in this country which were not pack-jammed with something between a hundred and fifty to two hundred different items, from dental floss to boracic acid, from razor blades to sodium perborate, from adhesive tape to coconut oil. Even the neatest wife will put off clearing out the medicine cabinet on the ground that she has something else to do that is more important at the moment, or more diverting. It was in the apartment of such a wife and her husband that I became enormously involved with a medicine cabinet one morning not long ago.

I had spent the week-end with this couple – they live on East Tenth Street near Fifth Avenue – such a weekend as left me reluctant to rise up on Monday morning with bright and shining face and go to work. They got up and went to work, but I didn't. I didn't get up until

about two-thirty in the afternoon. I had my face all lathered for shaving and the washbowl was full of hot water when suddenly I cut myself with the razor. I cut my ear. Very few men cut their ears with razors, but I do, possibly because I was taught the old Spencerian free-wrist movement by my writing teacher in the grammar grades. The ear bleeds rather profusely when cut with a razor and is difficult to get at. More angry than hurt, I jerked open the door of the medicine cabinet to see if I could find a styptic pencil and out fell, from the top shelf, a little black paper packet containing nine needles. It seems that this wife kept a little paper packet containing nine needles on the top shelf of the medicine cabinet. The packet fell into the soapy water of the wash-bowl, where the paper rapidly disintegrated, leaving nine needles at large in the bowl. I was, naturally enough, not in the best condition, either physical or mental, to recover nine needles from a washbowl. No gentleman who has lather on his face and whose ear is bleeding is in the best condition for anything, even something involving the handling of nine large blunt objects.

It did not seem wise to me to pull the plug out of the wash-bowl and let the needles go down the drain. I had visions of clogging up the plumbing system of the house, and also a vague fear of causing short circuits somehow or other (I know very little about electricity and I don't want to have it explained to me). Finally, I groped very gently around the bowl and eventually had four of the needles in the palm of one hand and three in the palm of the other – two I couldn't find. If I had thought quickly and clearly, I wouldn't have done that. A lathered man whose ear is bleeding and who has four wet needles in one hand and three in the other may be said to have reached the lowest known point of human efficiency. There is nothing he can do but stand there. I tried transferring the needles in my left hand to the palm of my right hand, but I couldn't get them off my left hand. Wet needles cling to you. In the end, I wiped the needles off on to a bath-towel which was hanging on a rod above the bath-tub. It was the only towel that I could find. I had to dry my hands afterwards on the bath-mat. Then I tried to find the needles in the towel. Hunting for seven needles in a bath-towel is the most tedious occupation I have engaged in. I could find only five of them. With the two that had been left in the bowl, that meant there were four needles in all missing – two in the wash-bowl and two others lurking in the towel or lying in the bath-tub under the towel. Frightful thoughts came to me of what might happen to anyone who used that towel or washed his face in the bowl or got into the tub, if I didn't find the missing needles. Well, I didn't find them. I sat down on the edge of the tub to think, and I decided finally that the only thing to do was wrap up the towel in a newspaper and take it away with me. I also decided to leave a note for my friends explaining as clearly as I could that I was afraid there were two

needles in the bath-tub and two needles in the wash-
bowl, and that they better be careful.

I looked everywhere in the apartment, but I could
not find a pencil, or a pen, or a typewriter. I could find
pieces of paper, but nothing with which to write on
them. I don't know what gave me the idea – a movie I
had seen, perhaps, or a story I had read – but I
suddenly thought of writing a message with a lipstick.
The wife might have an extra lipstick lying around and,
if so, I concluded it would be in the medicine cabinet.
I went back to the medicine cabinet and began poking
around in it for a lipstick. I saw what I thought looked
like the metal tip of one, and I got two fingers around
it and began to pull gently – it was under a lot of
things. Every object in the medicine cabinet began to
slide. Bottles broke in the wash-bowl and on the floor;
red, brown, and white liquids spurted; nail files, scissors,
razor blades, and miscellaneous objects sang and clat-
tered and tinkled. I was covered with perfume, per-
oxide, and cold cream.

It took me half an hour to get the debris all together
in the middle of the bathroom floor. I made no attempt
to put anything back in the medicine cabinet. I knew it
would take a steadier hand than mine and a less shat-
tered spirit. Before I went away (only partly shaved)
and abandoned the shambles, I left a note saying that I
was afraid there were needles in the bath-tub and the
wash-bowl and that I had taken their towel and that I
would call up and tell them everything – I wrote it in

iodine with the end of a toothbrush. I have not yet
called up, I am sorry to say. I have neither found the
courage nor thought up the words to explain what
happened. I suppose my friends believe that I deliberately smashed up their bathroom and stole their towel.
I don't know for sure, because they have not yet called
me up, either.

PHILIPPA PEARCE

What the Neighbours Did

Mum didn't like the neighbours, although – as we were the end cottage of the row – we only had one, really: Dirty Dick. Beyond him, the Macys.

Dick lived by himself – they said there used to be a wife, but she'd run away years ago; so now he lived as he wanted, which Mum said was like a pig in a pig-sty. Once I told Mum that I envied him, and she blew me up for it. Anyway, I'd have liked some of the things he had. He had two cars, although not for driving. He kept rabbits in one, and hens roosted in the other. He sold the eggs, which made part of his living. He made the rest from dealing in old junk (and in the village they said that he'd a stocking full of gold sovereigns which he kept under the mattress of his bed). Mostly he went about on foot, with his handcart for the junk; but he also rode a tricycle. The boys used to jeer at him sometimes, and once I asked him why he didn't ride a bicycle like everyone else. He said he liked a tricycle because you could go as slowly as you wanted, looking at things properly, without ever falling off.

Mrs Macy didn't like Dirty Dick any more than my mum did, but then she disliked everybody anyway. She didn't like Mr Macy. He was retired, and every morning in all weathers Mrs Macy'd turn him out into the garden and lock the door against him and make him stay there until he'd done as much work as she thought right. She'd put his dinner out to him through the scullery window. She couldn't bear to have anything alive about the place (you couldn't count old Macy himself, Dad used to say). That was one of the reasons why she didn't think much of us, with our dog and cat and Nora's two love-birds in a cage. Dirty Dick's hens and rabbits were even worse, of course.

Then the affair of the yellow dog made the Macys really hate Dirty Dick. It seems that old Mr Macy secretly got himself a dog. He never had any money of his own, because his wife made him hand it over, every week; so Dad reckoned that he must have begged the dog off someone who'd otherwise have had it destroyed.

The dog began as a secret, which sounds just about impossible, with Mrs Macy around. But every day Mr Macy used to take his dinner and eat it in his tool-shed, which opened on the side furthest from the house. That must have been his temptation; but none of us knew he'd fallen into it, until one summer evening we heard a most awful screeching from the Macy's house.

'That's old Ma Macy screaming,' said Dad, spreading his bread and butter.

'Oh, dear!' said Mum, jumping up and then sitting down again. 'Poor old Mr Macy!' But Mum was afraid of Mrs Macy. 'Run upstairs, boy, and see if you can see what's going on.'

So I did. I was just in time for the excitement, for, as I leaned out of the window, the Macy's back door flew open. Mr Macy came out first, with his head down and his arms sort of curved above it; and Mrs Macy came out close behind him, aiming at his head with a light broom – but aiming quite hard. She was screeching words, although it was difficult to pick out any of them. But some words came again and again, and I began to follow: Mr Macy had brought hairs with him into the house – short, curly, yellowish hairs, and he'd left those hairs all over the upholstery, and they must have come from a cat or a dog or a hamster or I don't know what, and so on and so on. Whatever the creature was, he'd been keeping it in the tool-shed, and turn it out he was going to, this very minute.

As usual Mrs Macy was right about what Mr Macy was going to do.

He opened the shed-door and out ambled a dog – a big, yellow-white old dog, looking a bit like a sheep, somehow, and about as quick-witted. As though it didn't notice what a tantrum Mrs Macy was in, it blundered gently towards her, and she lifted her broom high, and Mr Macy covered his eyes; and then Mrs Macy let out a real scream – a plain shriek – and dropped the broom and shot indoors and slammed the door after her.

The dog seemed puzzled, naturally; and so was I. It lumbered around towards Mr Macy, and then I saw its head properly, and that it had the most extraordinary eyes – like headlamps, somehow. I don't mean as big as headlamps, of course, but with a kind of whitish glare to them. Then I realized that the poor old thing must be blind.

The dog had raised its nose inquiringly towards Mr Macy, and Mr Macy had taken one timid, hopeful step towards the dog, when one of the sash windows of the house went up and Mrs Macy leaned out. She'd recovered from her panic, and she gave Mr Macy his orders. He was to take that disgusting animal and turn it out into the road, where he must have found it in the first place.

I knew that old Macy would be too dead scared to do anything else but what his wife told him.

I went down again to where the others were having tea. 'Well?' said Mum.

I told them, and I told them what Mrs Macy was making Mr Macy do to the blind dog. 'And if it's turned out like that on the road, it'll be killed by the first car that comes along.'

There was a pause, when even Nora seemed to be thinking; but I could see from their faces what they were thinking.

Dad said at last: 'That's bad. But we've four people in this little house, and a dog already, and a cat and two birds. There's no room for anything else.'

'But it'll be killed.'

'No,' said Dad. 'Not if you go at once, before any car comes, and take that dog down to the village, to the police-station. Tell them it's a stray.'

'But what'll they do with it?'

Dad looked as though he wished I hadn't asked that, but he said: 'Nothing, I expect. Well, they might hand it over to the Cruelty to Animals people.'

'And what'll they do with it?'

Dad was rattled. 'They do what they think best for animals – I should have thought they'd have taught you that at school. For goodness sake, boy!'

Dad wasn't going to say any more, nor Mum, who'd been listening with her lips pursed up. But everyone knew that the most likely thing was that an old, blind, ownerless dog would be destroyed.

But anything would be better than being run over and killed by a car just as you were sauntering along in the evening sunlight; so I started out of the house after the dog.

There he was, sauntering along, just as I'd imagined him. No sign of Mr Macy, of course: he'd have been called back indoors by his wife.

As I ran to catch up with the dog, I saw Dirty Dick coming home, and nearer the dog than I was. He was pushing his handcart, loaded with the usual bits of wood and other junk. He saw the dog coming and stopped, and waited; the dog came on hesitantly towards him.

'I'm coming for him,' I called.

'Ah,' said Dirty Dick. 'Yours?' He held out his hand towards the dog – the hand that my mother always said she could only bear to take hold of if the owner had to be pulled from certain death in a quicksand. Anyway, the dog couldn't see the colour of it, and it positively seemed to like the smell; it came on.

'No,' I said. 'Macys were keeping it, but Mrs Macy turned it out. I'm going to take it down to the police as a stray. What do you think they'll do with it?'

Dirty Dick never said much; this time he didn't answer. He just bent down to get his arm round the dog and in a second he'd hoisted him up on top of all the stuff in the cart. Then he picked up the handles and started off again.

So the Macys saw the blind dog come back to the row of cottages in state, as you might say, sitting on top of half a broken lavatory-seat on the very pinnacle of Dirty Dick's latest load of junk.

Dirty Dick took good care of his animals, and he took good care of this dog he adopted. It always looked well-fed and well-brushed. Sometimes he'd take it out with him, on the end of a long string; mostly he'd leave it comfortably at home. When it lay out in the back-garden, old Mr Macy used to look at it longingly over the fence. Once or twice I saw him poke his fingers through, towards what had once been his dog. But that had been for only a very short, dark time in the shed; and the old dog never moved towards the fingers. Then

'Macy!' his terrible old wife would call from the house, and he'd have to go.

Then suddenly we heard that Dirty Dick had been robbed – old Macy came round specially to tell us. 'An old sock stuffed with pound notes, that he kept up the bedroom chimney. Gone. Hasn't he told you?'

'No,' said Mum, 'but we don't have a lot to do with him.' She might have added that we didn't have a lot to do with the Macys either – I think this was the first time I'd ever seen one step over our threshold in a neighbourly way.

'You're thick with him sometimes,' said old Macy, turning on me. 'Hasn't he told you all about it?'

'Me?' I said. 'No.'

'Mind you, the whole thing's not to be wondered at,' said the old man. 'Front and back doors never locked, and money kept in the house. That's a terrible temptation to anyone with a weakness that way. A temptation that shouldn't have been put.'

'I dare say,' said Mum. 'It's a shame, all the same. His savings.'

'Perhaps the police'll be able to get it back for him,' I said. 'There'll be clues.'

The old man jumped – a nervous sort of jump. 'Clues? You think the police will find clues? I never thought of that. No, I did not. But has he gone to the police, anyway, I wonder. That's what I wonder. That's what I'm asking you.' He paused, and I realized that he meant me again. 'You're thick with him, boy.

Has he gone to the police? That's what I want to know . . .'

His mouth seemed to have filled with saliva, so that he had to stop to swallow, and couldn't say more. He was in a state, all right.

At that moment Dad walked in from work and wasn't best pleased to find that visitor instead of his tea waiting; and Mr Macy went.

Dad listened to the story over tea, and across the fence that evening he spoke to Dirty Dick and said he was sorry to hear about the money.

'Who told you?' asked Dirty Dick.

Dad said that old Macy had told us. Dirty Dick just nodded; he didn't seem interested in talking about it any more. Over that weekend no police came to the row, and you might have thought that old Macy had invented the whole thing, except that Dirty Dick had not contradicted him.

On Monday I was rushing off to school when I saw Mr Macy in their front garden, standing just between a big laurel bush and the fence. He looked straight at me and said 'Good morning' in a kind of whisper. I don't know which was odder – the whisper, or his wishing me good morning. I answered in rather a shout, because I was late and hurrying past. His mouth had opened as though he meant to say more, but then it shut, as though he'd changed his mind. That was all, that morning.

The next morning he was in just the same spot again,

and hailed me in the same way; and this time I was early, so I stopped.

He was looking shiftily about him, as though someone might be spying on us; but at least his wife couldn't be doing that, because the laurel bush was between him and their front windows. There was a tiny pile of yellow froth at one corner of his mouth, as though he'd been chewing his words over in advance. The sight of the froth made me want not to stay; but then the way he looked at me made me feel that I had to. No, it just made me; I had to.

'Look what's turned up in our back-garden,' he said, in the same whispering voice. And he held up a sock so dirty – partly with soot – and so smelly that it could only have been Dirty Dick's. It was stuffed full of something – pound notes, in fact. Old Macy's story of the robbery had been true in every detail.

I gaped at him.

'It's all to go back,' said Mr Macy. 'Back exactly to where it came from.' And then, as though I'd suggested the obvious – that he should hand the sock back to Dirty Dick himself with the same explanation just given to me: 'No, no. It must go back as though it had never been – never been taken away.' He couldn't use the word 'stolen'. 'Mustn't have the police poking round us. Mrs Macy wouldn't like it.' His face twitched at his own mention of her; he leaned forward. 'You must put it back boy. Put it back for me and keep your mouth shut. Go on. Yes.'

He must have been half out of his mind to think that I should do it, especially as I still didn't twig why. But as I stared at his twitching face I suddenly did understand. I mean, that old Macy had taken the sock, out of spite, and then lost his nerve.

He must have been half out of his mind to think that I would do that for him; and yet I did it. I took the sock and put it inside my jacket and turned back to Dirty Dick's cottage. I walked boldly up to the front door and knocked, and of course there was no answer. I knew he was already out with the cart.

There wasn't a sign of anyone looking, either from our house or the Macys'. (Mr Macy had already disappeared.) I tried the door and it opened, as I knew it would. I stepped inside and closed it behind me.

I'd never been inside before. The house was dirty, I suppose, and smelt a bit, but not really badly. It smelt of Dirty Dick and hens and rabbits — although it was untrue that he kept either hens or rabbits indoors, as Mrs Macy said. It smelt of dog, too, of course.

Opening straight off the living-room, where I stood, was the twisty, dark little stairway — exactly as in our cottage next door.

I went up.

The first room upstairs was full of junk. A narrow passageway had been kept clear to the second room, which opened off the first one. This was Dirty Dick's bedroom, with the bed unmade, as it probably was for weeks on end.

There was the fireplace, too, with a good deal of soot which had recently been brought down from the chimney. You couldn't miss seeing that – Dirty Dick couldn't have missed it, at the time. Yet he'd done nothing about his theft. In fact, I realized now that he'd probably said nothing either. The only person who'd let the cat out of the bag was poor old Macy himself.

I'd been working this out as I looked at the fireplace, standing quite still. Round me the house was silent. The only sound came from outside, where I could see a hen perched on the bumper of the old car in the back-garden, clucking for an egg newly laid. But when she stopped, there came another, tiny sound that terrified me: the click of a front-gate opening. Feet were clumping up to the front door . . .

I stuffed the sock up the chimney again, any old how, and was out of that bedroom in seconds; but on the threshold of the junk-room I stopped, fixed by the headlamp glare of the old blind dog. He must have been there all the time, lying under a three-legged washstand, on a heap of rags. All the time he would have been watching me, if he'd had his eyesight. He didn't move.

Meanwhile the front door had opened and the foot-steps had clumped inside, and stopped. There was a long pause, while I stared at the dog, who stared at me; and down below Dirty Dick listened and waited – he must have heard my movement just before.

At last: 'Well,' he called, 'why don't you come down?'

There was nothing else to do but go. Down that dark, twisty stair, knowing that Dirty Dick was waiting for me at the bottom. He was a big man, and strong. He heaved his junk about like nobody's business.

But when I got down, he wasn't by the foot of the stairs; he was standing by the open door, looking out, with his back to me. He hadn't been surprised to hear someone upstairs in his house, uninvited; but when he turned round from the doorway, I could see that he hadn't expected to see me. He'd expected someone else – old Macy, I suppose.

I wanted to explain that I'd only put the sock back – there was soot all over my hands, plain to be seen, of course – and that I'd had nothing to do with taking it in the first place. But he'd drawn his thick brows together as he looked at me, and he jerked his head towards the open door. I was frightened, and I went past him without saying anything. I was late for school now, anyway, and I ran.

I didn't see Dirty Dick again.

Later that morning Mum chose to give him a talking to, over the back fence, about locking his doors against pilferers in future. She says he didn't say he would, he didn't say he wouldn't; and he didn't say anything about anything having been stolen, or returned.

Soon after that, Mum saw him go out with the hand-cart with all his rabbits in a hutch, and he came back later without them. He did the same with his hens. We heard later that he'd given them away in the village; he hadn't even bothered to try and sell them.

Then he went round to Mum, wheeling the tricycle. He said he'd decided not to use it any more, and I could have it. He didn't leave any message for me.

Later still, Mum saw him set off for the third time that day with his handcart: not piled very high even, but with the old dog sitting on top. And that was the last that anyone saw of him.

He must have taken very little money with him: they found the sooty sock, still nearly full, by the rent-book on the mantelpiece. There was plenty to pay the rent due and to pay for cleaning up the house and the garden for the next tenant. He must have been fed up with being a householder, Dad said – and with having neighbours. He just wanted to turn tramp, and he did.

It was soon after he'd gone that I said to Mum that I envied him, and she blew me up, and went on and on about soap and water and fecklessness. All the same, I did envy him. I didn't even have the fun with his tricycle that he'd had. I never rode it, although I wanted to, because I was afraid that people I knew would laugh at me.

Harriet's Hairloom

'Oh, Mother,' Harriet said as she did every year. 'Can't I open my birthday presents at breakfast?'

And as she did every year, Mrs Armitage replied,

'Certainly not! You know perfectly well that you weren't born till half past four. You get your birthday presents at tea-time, not before.'

'We could change the custom now we're in our teens,' Harriet suggested cunningly. 'You know you hate having to get up at half past two in morning for Mark's presents.'

But Mark objected strongly to any change, and Mrs Armitage added,

'In any case, don't forget that as it's your thirteenth birthday you have to be shown into the Closed Room; there'd never be time to do that before school. Go and collect your schoolbooks now, and, Mark, wash the soot from behind your ears; if you must hunt for Lady Anne's pearls in the chimney, I wish you'd clean up before coming to breakfast.'

'You'd be as pleased as anyone else if I found them,' Mark grumbled, going off to put sooty marks all over the towels.

'What do you suppose is in the Closed Room?' Mark said later, as he and Harriet walked to the school bus. 'I think it's a rotten swindle that only girls in the family are allowed to go inside when they get to be thirteen. Suppose it's a monster like at Glamis, what'll you do?'

'Tame it,' said Harriet promptly. 'I shall feed it on bread-and-milk and lettuce.'

'That's hedgehogs, dope! Suppose it has huge teeth and tentacles and a poisonous sting three yards long?'

'Shut up! Anyway I don't suppose it is a monster. After all we never see Mother going into the Closed Room with bowls of food. It's probably just some mouldering old great-aunt in her coffin or something boring like that.'

Still, it was nice to have a Closed Room in the family, Harriet reflected, and she sat in the bus happily speculating about what it might contain – jewels, perhaps, rubies as big as tomatoes, or King Arthur's sword Excalibur, left with the Armitage family for safe keeping when he went off to Avalon, or the Welsh bard Taliesin, fallen asleep in the middle of a poem – or a Cockatrice – or the vanished crew of the *Marie Celeste*, playing cards and singing shanties—

Harriet was still in a dreamy state when school began. The first lesson was geography with old Mr Gubbins so there was no need to pay attention; she sat trying to think of suitable pet names for Cockatrices until she heard a stifled sobbing on her left.

'. . . is of course the Cathay of the ancients,' Mr

Gubbins was rambling on. 'Marco Polo in his travels . . .'

Harriet looked cautiously round and saw that her best friend, and left-hand neighbour Desiree, or Dizzry as everyone called her, was crying bitterly, hunched over the inkwell on her desk so that the tears ran into it.

Dizzry was the daughter of Ernie Perrow, the village chimney-sweep; the peculiarity of the Perrow family was that none of them ever grew to be more than six inches high. Dizzry travelled to school every day in Harriet's pocket and instead of sitting at her desk in the usual way had a small table and chair, which Mark had obligingly made her out of matchboxes, on the top of it.

'What's the matter?' whispered Harriet. 'Here, don't cry into the ink – you'll make it weaker than it is already. Haven't you a handkerchief?'

She pulled sewing things out of her own desk, snipped a shred off the corner of a tablecloth she was embroidering, and passed it to Dizzry, who gulped, nodded, took a deep breath, and wiped her eyes on it.

'What's the matter?' Harriet asked again.

'It was what Mr Gubbins said that started me off,' Dizzry muttered. 'Talking about Cathay. Our Min always used to say she'd a fancy to go to Cathay. She'd got it muddled up with café. She thought she'd get cake and raspberryade and ice-cream there.'

'Well, so what?' said Harriet, who saw nothing to cry about in that.

'Haven't you heard? We've lost her – we've lost our Min!'

'Oh, my goodness! You mean she's dead?'

'No, not died. Just lost. Nobody's seen her since yesterday breakfast time!'

Harriet privately thought this ought to have been rather a relief for the family but was too polite to say so. Min, the youngest of the Perrow children, was a perfect little fiend, always in trouble of one kind or another. When not engaged in entering sweet jars in the village shop and stealing Butter Kernels or Quince Drops, she was probably worming her way through keyholes and listening to people's secrets, or hitching a free lift round the houses in her enemy the postman's pocket and jabbing him with a darning needle as a reward for the ride, or sculling about the pond on Farmer Beezeley's ducks and driving them frantic by tickling them under their wings, or galloping down the street on somebody's furious collie, or climbing into the vicar's TV and frightening him half to death by shouting 'Time is short!' through the screen. She frequently ran fearful risks but seemed to have a charmed life. Everybody in the village heartily detested Min Perrow, but her elder brothers and sisters were devoted to her and rather proud of her exploits.

Poor Dizzry continued to cry, on and off, for the rest of the day. Harriet tried to console her but it seemed horribly probable that Min had at last gone too far and had been swallowed by a cow or drowned in a sump or rolled into a Swiss roll at the bakery while stealing jam – so many ill fates might easily have befallen her that it was hard to guess the likeliest.

'I'll help you hunt for her this evening,' Harriet promised, however, 'and so will Mark. As soon as my birthday tea's finished.'

Dizzry came home with Harriet for the birthday tea and was a little cheered by the cake made in the shape of a penguin with blackcurrant icing and an orange beak, and Harriet's presents, which included a do-it-yourself water-divining kit from Mark (a hazel twig and a bucket of water), an electronic guitar which could sing as well as play, a little pocket computer for working out sums and, from Harriet's fairy godmother, a tube of everlasting toothpaste. Harriet was not particularly grateful for this last; the thought of toothpaste supplied for the rest of her life left her unmoved.

'I'd rather have had an endless stick of liquorice,' she said crossly. 'Probably I shan't have any teeth left by the time I'm ninety; what use will toothpaste be then?'

Her presents from Dizzry were by far the nicest: a pink-and-orange necklace of spindleberries, beautifully carved, and a starling named Alastair whom Dizzry had trained to take messages, answer the telephone or the front door, and carry home small quantities of shopping.

'Now,' said Mrs Armitage rather nervously when the presents had been admired, 'I'd better show Harriet the Closed Room.'

Mr Armitage hurriedly retired to his study while Mark, controlling some natural feelings of envy, kindly said he would help Dizzry hunt for Min, and carried her off to inspect all the reapers and binders in Mr Beezeley's farmyard.

Harriet and Mrs Armitage went up to the attic floor and Mrs Armitage paused before a cobweb-shrouded door and pulled a rusty old key out of her pocket.

'Now you must say "I, Harriet Armitage, solemnly swear not to reveal the secret of this room to any other soul in the world." '

'But when I grow up and have a daughter,' objected Harriet, 'won't I have to tell her, just as Granny told you and you're telling me?'

'Well, yes, I suppose so,' Mrs Armitage said uncertainly. 'I've rather forgotten how the oath went, to tell you the truth.'

'Why do we have to promise not to tell?'

'To be honest, I haven't the faintest idea.'

'Let's skip that bit – there doesn't seem much point to it – and just go in,' Harriet suggested. So they opened the door (it was very stiff, for it had been shut at least twenty years) and went in.

The attic was dim, lit only by a patch of green glass tiles in the roof; it was quite empty except for a small, dusty loom, made of black wood, with a stool to match.

'A loom?' said Harriet, very disappointed. 'Is that all?'

'It isn't an ordinary loom,' her mother corrected her. 'It's a hairloom. For weaving human hair.'

'Who wants to weave human hair? What can you make?'

'I suppose you make a human hair mat. You must only use hair that's never been cut since birth.'

'Haven't you ever tried?'

'Oh, my dear, I never seemed to get a chance. When I was your age and Granny first showed me the loom everyone wore their hair short; you couldn't get a bit long enough to weave for love or money. And then you children came along – somehow I never found time.'

'Well I jolly well shall,' Harriet said. 'I'll try and get hold of some hair. I wonder if Miss Pring would let me have hers? I bet it's never been cut – she must have yards. Maybe you can make a cloak of invisibility, or the sort that turns swans into humans.'

She was so pleased with this notion that only as they went downstairs did she think to ask, 'How did the loom get into the family?'

'I'm a bit vague about that,' Mrs Armitage admitted. 'I believe it belonged to a Greek ancestress that one of the crusading Armitages married and brought back to England. She's the one I'm called Penelope after.'

Without paying much attention, Harriet went off to find Mark and Dizzry. Her father said they were along at the church, so she followed, pausing at the post office to ask elderly Miss Pring the postmistress if she would sell her long grey hair to be woven into a rug.

'It would look very pretty,' she coaxed. 'I could dye some of it pink or blue.'

Miss Pring was not keen.

'Sell my hair? Cut it off? The idea! Dye it? What impertinence! Get along with you, sauce-box!'

So Harriet had to abandon that scheme, but she stuck up a postcard on the notice-board: HUMAN HAIR REQUIRED, UNCUT: BEST PRICES PAID, and posted off another to the local paper. Then she joined Mark and Dizzry, who were searching the church organ pipes, but without success.

Harriet had met several other members of the Perrow family on her way: Ernie, Min's father, driving an old dolls' push-chair which he had fitted with an engine and turned into a convertible like a Model T Ford; old Gran Perrow, stomping along and gloomily shouting 'Min!' down all the drain-holes; and Sid, one of the boys, riding a bike made from cocoa tins and poking out nests from the hedge with a bamboo in case Min had been abducted.

When it was too dark to go on searching Harriet and Mark left Dizzry at Rose Cottage, where the Perrows lived.

'We'll go on looking tomorrow!' they called. And Harriet said, 'Don't worry too much.'

'I expect she'll be all right wherever she is,' Mark said. 'I'd back Min against a mad bull any day.'

As they walked home he asked Harriet,

'What about the Closed Room, then? Any monster?'

'No, very dull – just a hairloom.'

'I say, you shouldn't tell me, should you?'

'It's all right – we agreed to skip the promise to keep it secret.'

'What a let-down,' Mark said. 'Who wants an old loom?'

They arrived home to trouble. Their father was complaining, as he did every day, about soot on the carpets and black tide-marks on the bathroom basin and towels.

'Well, if you don't want me to find Lady Anne's necklace—' Mark said aggrievedly. 'If it was worth a thousand pounds when she lost it in 1660, think what it would fetch now.'

'Why in heaven's name would it be up the chimney? Stop arguing and go to bed. And brush your teeth!'

'I'll lend you some of my toothpaste,' Harriet said.

'Just the same,' Mark grumbled, brushing his teeth with yards of toothpaste so that the foam stood out on either side of his face like Dundreary whiskers and flew all over the bathroom, 'Ernie Perrow definitely told me that his great-great-great-grandfather Oliver Perrow had a row with Lady Anne Armitage because she ticked him off for catching field-mice in her orchard; Oliver was the village sweep, and her pearls vanished just after; Ernie thinks old Oliver stuck them in the chimney to teach her a lesson, and then he died, eaten by a fox before he had a chance to tell anyone. But Ernie's sure that's where the pearls are.'

'Perhaps Min's up there looking for them too.'

'Not her! She'd never do anything as useful as that.'

Harriet had asked Alastair the starling to call her at seven; in fact she was roused at half past six by loud bangs on the front door.

'For heaven's sake, somebody, tell that maniac to go away!' shouted Mr Armitage from under his pillow.

Harriet flung on a dressing-gown and ran downstairs. What was her surprise to find at the door a little old man in a white duffel-coat with the hood up. He carried a very large parcel, wrapped in sacking. Harriet found the sharp look he gave her curiously disconcerting.

'Would it be Miss Armitage now, the young lady who put the advertisement in the paper then?'

'About hair?' Harriet said eagerly. 'Yes, I did. Have you got some, Mr—?'

'Mr Thomas Jones, the Druid, I am. Beautiful hair I have then, look you – finer than any lady's in the land. Only see now till I get this old parcel undone!' And he dumped the bundle down at her feet and started unknotting the cords. Harriet helped. When the last half-hitch twanged apart a great springy mass of hair came boiling out. It was soft and fine, dazzlingly white with just a few strands of black, and smelt slightly of tobacco.

'There, now indeed to goodness! Did you ever see finer?'

'But,' said Harriet, 'has it ever been cut short?' She very much hoped that it had not; it seemed impossible that they would ever be able to parcel it up again.

'Never has a scissor-blade been laid to it, till I cut it all off last night,' the old man declared.

Harriet wondered whose it was; something slightly malicious and self-satisfied about the old man's grin as he said, 'I cut it all off' prevented her from asking.

'Er – how much would you want for it?' she inquired cautiously.

'Well, indeed,' he said. 'It would be hard to put a price on such beautiful hair, whatever.'

At this moment there came an interruption. A large van drew up in front of the Armitage house. On its sides iridescent bubbles were painted, and, in rainbow colours, the words SUGDEN'S SOAP.

A uniformed driver jumped out, consulting a piece of paper.

'Mr Mark Armitage live here?' he asked Harriet. She nodded.

'Will he take delivery of one bathroom, complete with shower, tub, footbath, de-luxe basin, plastic curtains, turkish towelling, chrome sponge-holder, steel-and-enamel hair drier, and a six years' supply of Sugden's Soap?'

'I suppose so,' Harriet said doubtfully. 'You're sure there's no mistake?'

The delivery note certainly had Mark's name and address.

'Mark!' Harriet yelled up the stairs, forgetting it was still only seven a.m. 'Did you order a bathroom? Because it's come.'

'Merciful goodness!' groaned the voice of Mr Armitage. 'Has no one any consideration for my hours of rest?'

Mark came running down, looking slightly embarrassed.

'Darn it,' he said as he signed the delivery note, 'I never expected I'd get a bathroom; I was hoping for the free cruise to Saposoa.'

'Where shall we put it, guv?' said the driver, who was plainly longing to be away and get some breakfast at the nearest carmen's pull-in.

Mark looked about him vaguely. At this moment Mr Armitage came downstairs in pyjamas and a very troublesome frame of mind.

'Bathroom? Bathroom?' he said. 'You've bought a bathroom? What the blazes did you want to go and get a bathroom for? Isn't the one we have good enough for you, pray? You leave it dirty enough. Who's going to pay for this? And why has nobody put the kettle on?'

'I won it,' Mark explained, blushing. 'It was the second prize in the Sugden's Soap competition. In the *Radio Times*, you know.'

'What did you have to do?' Harriet asked.

'Ten uses for soap in correct order of importance.'

'I bet washing came right at the bottom,' growled his father. 'Greased stairs and fake soft-centres are more your mark.'

'Anyway he won!' Harriet pointed out. 'Was that all you had to do?'

'You had to write a couplet too.'

'What was yours?'

Mark blushed even pinker. 'Rose or White or

Heliotrope, Where there's life there's Sugden's Soap.'

'Come on now,' said the van driver patiently, 'we don't want to be here all day, do we? Where shall we put it, guv? In the garden?'

'Certainly not,' snapped Mr Armitage. He was proud of his garden.

'How about in the field?' suggested Harriet diplomatically. 'Then Mark and I can wash in it, and you needn't be upset by soot on the towels.'

'That's true,' he father said, brightening a little. 'All right, stick it in the field. And now will somebody please put on a kettle and make a cup of tea, is that too much to ask?' And he stomped back to bed, leaving Mark and the driver to organize the erection of the bathroom in the field beside the house. Harriet put a kettle on the stove and went back to Mr Jones the Druid who was sunning himself in the front porch.

'Have you decided what you want for your hair?' she asked.

'Oh,' he said. 'There is a grand new bathroom you have with you! Lucky that is, indeed. Now I am thinking I do not want any money at all for my fine bundle of hair, but only to strike a bargain with you.'

'Very well,' Harriet said cautiously.

'No bathroom I have at my place, see? Hard it is to wash the old beard, and chilly of a winter morning in the stream. But if you and your brother, that I can see is a kind-hearted obliging young gentleman, would let me come and give it a bit of a lather now and again in your bathroom—'

'Why yes, of course,' Harriet said. 'I'm sure Mark won't mind at all.'

'So it shall be, then. Handy that will be, indeed. Terrible deal of the old beard there is, look you, and grubby she do get.'

With that he undid his duffel-coat and pulled back the hood. All round his head and wound about his body like an Indian Sari was a prodigiously long white beard which he proceeded to untwine until it trailed on the ground. It was similar to the white hair in the bundle, but not so clean.

'Is that somebody's beard, then?' Harriet asked, pointing to the bundle.

'My twin brother, Dai Jones the Bard. Bathroom he has by him, the lucky old cythryblwr! But soon I will be getting a bigger one. Made a will, my Dad did, see, leaving all his money to the one of us who has the longest and whitest beard on our ninetieth birthday, that falls tomorrow on Midsummer Day. So I crept into his house last night and cut his beard off while he slept; hard he'll find it now to grow another in time! All Dada's money I will be getting, he, he, he!'

Mr Jones the Druid chuckled maliciously.

Harriet could not help thinking he was rather a wicked old man, but a bargain was a bargain, so she picked up the bundle of beard, with difficulty, and was about to say goodbye when he stopped her.

'Weaving the hair into a mat, you would be, isn't it?'

he said wheedlingly. 'There is a fine bath-mat it would make! Towels and curtains there are in that grand new bathroom of yours but no bath-mat — pity that is, indeed.' He gave her a cunning look out of the corners of his eyes, but Harriet would not commit herself.

'Come along this evening, then, I will, for a good old wash-up before my birthday,' Mr Jones said. He wound himself in his beard again and went off with many nods and bows. Harriet ran to the field to see how the bathroom was getting on. Mark had it nearly finished. True enough, there was no bath-mat. It struck Harriet that Mr Jones's suggestion was not a bad one.

'I'll start weaving a mat as soon as we've had another thorough hunt for Min Perrow,' she said. 'Saturday, thank goodness, no school.'

However during breakfast (which was late, owing to these various events) Ernie Perrow drove along in the push-chair with Lily and Dizzry to show the Armitages an air letter which had arrived from the British Consul in Cathay.

Dear Sir or Madam,

Kindly make earliest arrangements to send passage money back to England for your daughter Hermione who has had herself posted here, stowed away in a box of Health Biscuits. Please forward without delay fare and expenses totalling £1,093 7s. 1d.

A postscript, scrawled by Min, read: 'Dun it at last! Sux to silly old postmun!'

'Oh, what shall we do?' wept Mrs Perrow. 'A thousand pounds! How can we ever find it?'

While the grown-ups discussed ways and means, Mark went back to his daily search for Lady Anne's pearls, and Harriet took the woebegone Dizzry up to the attic, hoping to distract her by a look at the hairloom.

Dizzry was delighted with it. 'Do let's do some weaving!' she said. 'I like weaving better than anything.'

So Harriet lugged in the great bundle of beard and they set up the loom. Dizzry was an expert weaver. She had been making beautiful scarves for years on a child's toy loom – she could nip to and fro with the shuttle almost faster than Harriet's eyes could follow. By teatime they had woven a handsome thick white mat with the words BATH MA across the middle (there had not been quite enough black for the final T).

'Anyway you can see what it's meant to be,' Harriet said. They took the new mat and spread it in their elegant bathroom.

'Tell you what,' Mark said, 'we'd better hide the bath and basin plugs when Min gets back or she'll climb in and drown herself.'

'Oh, I do wonder what Dad and Mum are doing about getting her back,' sighed Dizzry, who was sitting on a sponge. She wiped her eyes on a corner of Harriet's face-cloth.

'Let's go along to your house,' Harriet said, 'and find out.'

There was an atmosphere of deep gloom in the Perrow household. Ernie had arranged to sell his Model T push-chair, the apple of his eye, to the Motor Museum at Beaulieu.

'A thousand pounds they say they'll give for it,' he said miserably. 'With that and what I've saved from the chimney sweeping, we can just about pay the fare. Won't I half clobber young Min when I get her back, the little varmint!'

'Mrs Perrow,' Harriet said, 'may Dizzry come and spend the evening at our house, as Mother and Daddy are going to a dance? And have a bath in our new bathroom? Mother says it's all right and I'll take great care of her.'

'Oh, very well, if your Ma doesn't mind,' sighed Mrs Perrow. 'I'm so distracted I hardly know if I'm coming or going. Don't forget your wash things, Diz, and the bath-salts.'

Harriet was enchanted with the bath-salts, no bigger than hundreds-and-thousands.

On Midsummer Eve the Armitage children were allowed to stay up as late as they liked. Mark, a single-minded boy, said he intended to go on hunting for Lady Anne's necklace in the chimney. The girls had their baths and then went up to Harriet's room with a bagful of apples and the gramophone, intending to have a good gossip.

At half past eleven Harriet, happening to glance out of the window, saw a light in the field.

'That must be Mr Jones,' she said. 'I'd forgotten he was coming to shampoo his beard. It's not Mark, I can still hear him bumping around in the chimney.'

There was indeed an excited banging to be heard from the chimney-breast, but it was as nothing compared with the terrible racket that suddenly broke out in the field. They heard shouts and cries of rage, thuds, crashes, and the tinkle of smashed glass.

'Heavens, what can be going on?' cried Harriet. She flung up the sash and prepared to climb out of the window.

'Wait for me!' said Dizzry.

'Here, jump into my pocket. Hold tight!'

Harriet slid down the wisteria and dashed across the garden. A moment later they arrived at the bathroom door and witnessed a wild scene.

Evidently Mr Jones the Druid had finished washing his beard and been about to leave when he saw his doom waiting for him outside the door in the form of another, very angry, old man who was trying to batter his way in.

'It must be his brother!' Harriet whispered. 'Mr Jones the Bard!'

The second old man had no beard, only a ragged white frill cut short round his chin. He was shouting.

'Wait till I catch you, you hocsdwr, you herwhaliwr, you ffrawddunio, you wicked old llechwr! A snake would think shame to spit on you! Cutting off your brother's beard, indeed! Just let me get at you and I'll trim you to spillikins. I'll shave your beard round your eyebrows!' And he beat on the door with a huge pair of shears. A pane of glass fell in and broke on the bathroom tiles; then the whole door gave way.

Dizzry left Harriet's pocket and swarmed up on to her head to see what was happening. They heard a fearful bellow from inside the bathroom, a stamping and crashing, fierce grunts, the hiss of the shower and more breaking glass.

'Hey!' Harriet shouted. 'Stop wrecking our bathroom!'

No answer. The noise of battle went on.

Then the bathroom window flew open and Jones the Druid shot out, all tangled in his beard which was snowy white now, but still damp. He had the bath-mat rolled up under his arm. As soon as he was out he flung it down, leapt on it, and shouted, 'Take me out of here!'

The mat took off vertically and hovered, about seven feet up, while Mr Jones began hauling in his damp beard, hand over hand. 'Come back!' Harriet cried. 'You've no right to go off with our bath-mat.'

Jones the Bard came roaring out of the window, waving his shears.

'Come back, ystraffaldiach! Will you come down off there and let me mince you into macaroni! Oh, you wicked old weasel, I'll trim your beard shorter than an earwig's toe-nails!'

He made a grab for the bath-mat but it was just out of reach.

'He, he, he!' cackled Jones the Druid up above. 'You didn't know your fine beard would make up so nice into a flying carpet, did you, brother? Has to be woven on a hair-loom on Midsummer Eve and then it'll carry you faster than the Aberdovey Flyer.'

'Just let me get at you, rheibiwr!' snarled Jones the Bard, making another vain grab.

But Dizzry, who was now jumping up and down on the top of Harriet's head, made a tremendous spring, grabbed hold of a trailing strand of Mr Jones's beard, and hauled herself up on to a corner of the flying bath-mat.

'Oh dammo!' gasped the Druid at the sight of her. He was so taken aback that he lost his balance, staggered, and fell headlong on top of his brother. There was a windmill confusion of arms and legs, all swamped by the foaming mass of beard. Then Jones the Bard grabbed his shears with a shout of triumph and began chopping away great sways of white hair.

Harriet, however, paid no heed to these goings-on.

'Dizzry!' she shouted, cupping her hands round her mouth. 'It's a wishing-mat. Make it take you–'

Dizzry nodded. She needed no telling. 'Take me to Cathay!' she cried, and the mat soared away through the milky air of midsummer night.

At this moment Mark came running across the field.

'Oh, Mark!' Harriet burst out. 'Look what those old fiends have done to our bathroom! It's ruined. They ought to be made to pay for it.'

Mark glanced through the broken window. The place was certainly a shambles: bath and basin were both smashed, the sponge-rack was wrapped round the hair-drier, the towels were trodden into a soggy pulp and the curtains were in ribbons.

The Jones brothers were in equally bad shape. Jones the Bard was kneeling on Jones the Druid's stomach; he had managed to trim every shred of hair off his brother's head, but he himself was as bald as a coot. Both had black eyes and swollen lips.

'Oh, well,' Mark said. 'They seem to have trouble of their own. I bet neither of them comes into that legacy now. And I never did care much for washing anyway. Look, here comes Dizzry back.'

The bath-mat swooped to a three-point landing, Dizzry and Min rolled off it, laughing and crying.

'You wicked, wicked, bad little girl,' Dizzry cried, shaking and hugging her small sister at the same time. 'Don't you ever dare do such a thing again.'

'Now I will take my own property which is my lawful beard,' said Mr Jones the Bard, and he jumped off his brother's stomach on to the mat and addressed it in a flood of Welsh, which it evidently understood, for it rose into the air and flew off in a westerly direction. Mr Jones the Druid slunk away across the field looking, Dizzry said, as hangdog as a cat that has fallen into the milk.

'Now we've lost our bath-mat,' Harriet sighed.

'I'll help you make another,' Dizzry said. 'There's

plenty of hair lying about. And at least we've got Min back.'

'Was it nice in Cathay, Min?' Mark said.

'Smashing. I had rice-cake and cherry ice and Coca-Cola.'

At this point Mr and Mrs Armitage returned from their dance and kindly drove Dizzry and Min to break the joyful news to their parents.

Harriet and Mark had a try at putting the bathroom to rights, but it was really past hope.

'I must say, trouble certainly haunts this household,' remarked Mr Armitage, when he came back and found them at it. 'Hurry up and get to bed, you two. Do you realize it's four o'clock on midsummer morning? Oh, Lord, I suppose now we have to go back to the old regime of sooty footmarks all over the bathroom.'

'Certainly not,' said Mark. 'I'd forgotten to tell you. I found Lady Anne's pearls.'

He pulled them out and dangled them: a soot-black, six-foot double strand of pearls as big as cobnuts, probably worth a king's ransom.

'Won't Ernie Perrow be pleased to know they really were in the chimney?' he said.

'Oh, get to bed!' snapped his father. 'I'm fed up with hearing about the Perrows.'

The Truth About Pyecraft

He sits not a dozen yards away. If I glance over my shoulder I can see him. And if I catch his eye – and usually I catch his eye – it meets me with an expression–

It is mainly an imploring look – and yet with suspicion in it.

Confound his suspicion! If I wanted to tell on him I should have told long ago. I don't tell and I don't tell, and he ought to feel at his ease. As if anything so gross and fat as he could feel at ease! Who would believe me if I did tell?

Poor old Pyecraft! Great, uneasy jelly of substance! The fattest clubman in London.

He sits at one of the little club tables in the huge bay by the fire, stuffing. What is he stuffing? I glance judiciously and catch him biting at the round of hot buttered teacake, with his eyes on me. Confound him! – with his eyes on me!

That settles it, Pyecraft! Since you will be abject, since you will behave as though I was not a man of honour, here, right under your embedded eyes, I write the thing down – the plain truth about Pyecraft. The man I helped, the man I shielded, and who has requited me by making my club unendurable, absolutely unendurable, with his liquid appeal, with the perpetual 'don't tell' of his looks.

And, besides, why does he keep on eternally eating?

Well, here goes for the truth, the whole truth, and nothing but the truth!

Pyecraft – I made the acquaintance of Pyecraft in this very smoking-room. I was a young, nervous new member, and he saw it. I was sitting all alone, wishing I knew more of the members, and suddenly he came, a great rolling front of chins and abdomina, towards me, and grunted and sat down in a chair close by me and wheezed for a space, and scraped for a space with a match and lit a cigar, and then addressed me. I forget what he said – something about the matches not lighting properly, and afterwards as he talked he kept stopping the waiters one by one as they went by, and telling them about the matches in that thin, fluty voice he has. But, anyhow, it was in some such way we began our talking.

He talked about various things and came round to games. And thence to my figure and complexion. 'You ought to be a good cricketer,' he said. I am slender, slender to what some people would call lean, and I am rather dark, having a Hindu great-grandmother.

But he only talked about me in order to get to himself.

'I expect,' he said, 'you take no more exercise than I do, and you probably eat no less.' (Like all excessively obese people he fancied he ate nothing.) 'Yet' – and he smiled an oblique smile – 'we differ.'

And then he began to talk about his fatness and his fatness; and all he did for his fatness and all he was going to do for his fatness; what people had advised him to do for his fatness and what he had heard of people doing for fatness similar to his. 'A priori,' he said, 'one would think a question of nutrition could be answered by dietary and a question of assimilation by drugs.' It was stifling. It was dumpling talk. It made me feel swelled to hear him.

One stands that sort of thing once in a way at a club, but a time came when I fancied I was standing too much. He took to me altogether too conspicuously. I could never go into the smoking-room but he would come wallowing towards me, and sometimes he came and gormandized round and about me while I had my lunch. He seemed at times almost to be clinging to me. He was a bore, but not so fearful a bore as to be limited to me; and from the first there was something in his manner – almost as though he knew, almost as though he penetrated to the fact that I might – that there was a remote, exceptional chance in me that no one else presented.

'I'd give anything to get it down,' he would say – 'anything,' and peer at me over his vast cheeks and pant.

Poor old Pyecraft! He has just gonged, no doubt to order another buttered teacake!

He came to the actual thing one day. 'Our Pharmacopoeia,' he said, 'our Western Pharmacopoeia, is anything but the last word of medical science. In the East, I've been told–'

He stopped and stared at me. It was like being at an aquarium.

I was quite suddenly angry with him. 'Look here,' I said, 'who told you about my great-grandmother's recipes?'

'Well,' he fenced.

'Every time we've met for a week,' I said, 'and we've met pretty often – you've given me a broad hint or so about that little secret of mine.'

'Well,' he said, 'now the cat's out of the bag, I'll admit, yes, it is so. I had it–'

'From Pattison?'

'Indirectly,' he said, which I believe was lying, 'yes.'

'Pattison,' I said, 'took that stuff at his own risk.'

He pursed his mouth and bowed.

'My great-grandmother's recipes,' I said, 'are queer things to handle. My father was near making me promise–'

'He didn't?'

'No. But he warned me. He himself used one – once.'

'Ah! . . . But do you think–? Suppose – suppose there did happen to be one–'

'The things are curious documents,' I said. 'Even the smell of 'em . . . No!'

But after going so far Pyecraft was resolved I should go farther. I was always a little afraid if I tried his patience too much he would fall on me suddenly and smother me. I own I was weak. But I was also annoyed with Pyecraft. I had got to that state of feeling for him that disposed me to say, 'Well, take the risk!' The little affair of Pattison to which I have alluded was a different matter altogether. What it was doesn't concern us now, but I knew, anyhow, that the particular recipe I used then was safe. The rest I didn't know so much about, and, on the whole, I was inclined to doubt their safety pretty completely.

Yet even if Pyecraft got poisoned–

I must confess the poisoning of Pyecraft struck me as an immense undertaking.

That evening I took that queer, odd-scented sandal-wood box out of my safe and turned the rustling skins over. The gentleman who wrote the recipes for my great-grandmother evidently had a weakness for skins of a miscellaneous origin, and his hand-writing was cramped to the last degree. Some of the things are quite unreadable to me – though my family, with its Indian Civil Service associations, had kept up a knowledge of Hindustani from generation to generation – and none are absolutely plain sailing. But I found the one that I knew was there soon enough, and sat on the floor by my safe for some time looking at it.

'Look here,' said I to Pyecraft next day, and snatched the slip away from his eager grasp.

'So far as I can make it out, this is a recipe for Loss of Weight. ('Ah!' said Pyecraft.) I'm not absolutely sure, but I think it's that. And if you take my advice you'll leave it alone.'

'Let me try it,' said Pyecraft.

I leant back in my chair. My imagination made one mighty effort and fell flat within me. 'What in heaven's name, Pyecraft,' I asked, 'do you think you'll look like when you get thin?'

He was impervious to reason. I made him promise never to say a word to me about his disgusting fatness again whatever happened – never, and then I handed him that little piece of skin.

'It's nasty stuff,' I said.

'No matter,' he said, and took it.

He goggled at it. 'But, but–' he said.

He had just discovered that it wasn't English.

'To the best of my ability,' I said, 'I will do you a translation.'

I did my best. After that we didn't speak for a fortnight. Whenever he approached me I frowned and motioned him away, and he respected our compact, but at the end of the fortnight he was as fat as ever. And then he got a word in.

'I must speak,' he said. 'It isn't fair. There's something wrong. It's done me no good. You're not doing your great-grandmother justice.'

'Where's the recipe?'

He produced it gingerly from his pocket-book.

I ran my eye over the items. 'Was the egg addled?' I asked.

'No. Ought it to have been?'

'That,' I said, 'goes without saying in all my poor dear great-grandmother's recipes. When condition or quality is not specified you must get the worst. She was drastic or nothing . . . And there's one or two possible alternatives to some of these other things. You got fresh rattlesnake venom?'

'I got rattlesnake from Jamrach's. It cost – it cost–'

'That's your affair, anyhow. This last item–'

'I know a man who–'

'Yes. H'm. Well, I'll write the alternatives down. So far as I know the language, the spelling of this recipe is particularly atrocious. By-the-bye, dog here probably means pariah dog.'

For a month after that I saw Pyecraft constantly at the club and as fat and anxious as ever. He kept our treaty, but at times he broke the spirit of it by shaking his head despondently. Then one day in the cloak-room he said, 'Your great-grandmother–'

'Not a word against her,' I said: and he held his peace.

I could have fancied he had desisted, and I saw him one day talking to three new members about his fatness as though he was in search of other recipes. And then, quite unexpectedly, his telegram came.

'Mr Formalyn!' bawled a page-boy under my nose and I took the telegram and opened it at once.

'For heaven's sake come – Pyecraft.'

'H'm,' said I, and to tell the truth I was so pleased at the rehabilitation of my great-grandmother's reputation this evidently promised that I made a most excellent lunch.

I got Pyecraft's address from the hall porter. Pyecraft inhabited the upper half of a house in Bloomsbury, and I went there as soon as I had done my coffee and Trappistine. I did not wait to finish my cigar.

'My Pyecraft?' said I, at the front door.

They believed he was ill; he hadn't been out for two days.

'He expects me,' said I, and they sent me up.

I rang the bell at the lattice-door upon the landing.

'He shouldn't have tried it, anyhow,' I said to myself. 'A man who eats like a pig ought to look like a pig.'

An obviously worthy woman, with an anxious face and a carelessly placed cap, came and surveyed me through the lattice.

I gave my name and she opened his door for me in a dubious fashion.

'Well?' said I, as we stood together inside Pyecraft's piece of the landing.

' 'E said you was to come in if you came,' she said, and regarded me, making no motion to show me anywhere. And then, confidentially, ' 'E's locked in, sir.'

'Locked in?'

'Locked himself in yesterday morning and 'asn't let anyone in since, sir. And ever and again swearing. Oh, my!'

I stared at the door she indicated by her glances. 'In there?' I said.

'Yes, sir.'

'What's up?'

She shook her head sadly. ' 'E keeps on calling for vittles, sir. 'Eavy vittles 'e wants. I get 'im what I can. Pork 'e's 'ad, sooit puddin', sossiges, noo bread. Everything like that. Left outside, if you please, and me go away. 'E's eatin', sir, somethink awful.'

There came a piping bawl from inside the door: 'That Formalyn?'

'That you, Pyecraft?' I shouted, and went and banged the door.

'Tell her to go away.'

I did.

Then I could hear a curious pattering upon the door, almost like someone feeling for the handle in the dark, and Pyecraft's familiar grunts.

'It's all right,' I said, 'she's gone.'

But for a long time the door didn't open.

I heard the key turn. Then Pyecraft's voice said, 'Come in.'

I turned the handle and opened the door. Naturally I expected to see Pyecraft.

Well, you know, he wasn't there!

I never had such a shock in my life. There was his sitting-room in a state of untidy disorder. Plates and dishes among the books and writing things, and several chairs overturned, but Pyecraft——

'It's all right, o' man; shut the door,' he said, and then I discovered him.

There he was right up close to the cornice in the corner by the door, as though someone had glued him to the ceiling. His face was anxious and angry. He panted and gesticulated. 'Shut the door,' he said. 'If that woman gets hold of it–'

I shut the door, and went and stood away from him and stared.

'If anything gives way and you tumble down,' I said, 'you'll break your neck, Pyecraft.'

'I wish I could,' he wheezed.

'A man of your age and weight getting up to kiddish gymnastics–'

'Don't,' he said, and looked agonized. 'Your damned great-grandmother–'

'Be careful,' I warned him.

'I'll tell you,' he said, and gesticulated.

'How the deuce,' said I, 'are you holding on up there?'

And then abruptly I realized that he was not holding on at all, that he was floating up there – just as a gas-filled bladder might have floated in the same position. He began a struggle to thrust himself away from the ceiling and to clamber down the wall to me. 'It's that prescription,' he panted, as he did so. 'Your great-gran–'

'No!' I cried.

He took hold of a framed engraving rather carelessly as he spoke and it gave way, and he flew back to the ceiling again, while the picture smashed on to the sofa. Bump he went against the ceiling, and I knew then why he was all over white on the more salient curves and angles of his person. He tried again more carefully, coming down by way of the mantel.

It was really a most extraordinary spectacle, that great, fat, apoplectic-looking man upside down and trying to get from the ceiling to the floor. 'That pre-scription,' he said. 'Too successful.'

'How?'

'Loss of weight, almost complete.'

And then, of course, I understood.

'By jove, Pyecraft,' said I, 'what you wanted was a cure for fatness! But you always called it weight. You would call it weight.'

Somehow I was extremely delighted. I quite liked Pyecraft for the time. 'Let me help you!' I said, and took his hand and pulled him down. He kicked about, trying to get foothold somewhere. It was very like hold-ing a flag on a windy day.

'That table,' he said, pointing, 'is solid mahogany and very heavy. If you can put me under that–'

I did, and there he wallowed about like a captive balloon, while I stood on his hearthrug and talked to him.

I lit a cigar. 'Tell me,' I said, 'what happened?'

'I took it,' he said.

'How did it taste?'

'Oh, beastly!'

I should fancy they all did. Whether one regards the ingredients or the probable compound or the possible results, almost all my great-grandmother's remedies appear to me at least to be extraordinarily uninviting. For my own part—

'I took a little sip first.'

'Yes?'

'And as I felt lighter and better after an hour, I decided to take the draught.'

'My dear Pyecraft!'

'I held my nose,' he explained. 'And then I kept on getting lighter and lighter – and helpless, you know.'

He gave way suddenly to a burst of passion. 'What the goodness am I to do?' he said.

'There's one thing pretty evident,' I said, 'that you mustn't do. If you go out of doors you'll go up and up.' I waved an arm upward. 'They'd have to send Santos-Dumont after you to bring you down again.'

'I suppose it will wear off?'

I shook my head. 'I don't think you can count on that,' I said.

And then there was another burst of passion, and he kicked out at adjacent chairs and banged the floor. He behaved just as I should have expected a great, fat, self-indulgent man to behave under trying circumstances – that is to say, very badly. He spoke of me and of my great-grandmother with an utter want of discretion.

'I never asked you to take the stuff,' I said.

And generously disregarding the insults he was putting upon me, I sat down in his armchair and began to talk to him in a sober, friendly fashion.

I pointed out to him that this was a trouble he had brought upon himself, and that it had almost an air of poetical justice. He had eaten too much. This he disputed, and for a time we argued the point.

He became noisy and violent, so I desisted from this aspect of his lesson. 'And then,' said I, 'you committed the sin of euphemism. You called it, not Fat, which is just and inglorious, but Weight. You–'

He interrupted to say that he recognized all that. What was he to do?

I suggested he should adapt himself to his new conditions. So we came to the really sensible part of the business. I suggested that it would not be difficult for him to learn to walk about on the ceiling with his hands–

'I can't sleep,' he said.

But that was no great difficulty. It was quite possible, I pointed out, to make a shake-up under a wire mattress, fasten the under things on with tapes, and have a blanket, sheet, and coverlid to button at the side. He would have to confide in his housekeeper, I said; and after some squabbling he agreed to that. (Afterwards it was quite delightful to see the beautifully matter-of-fact way with which the good lady took all these amazing inversions.) He could have a library ladder in his room, and all his meals could be laid on the top of his bookcase. We also hit on an ingenious device by which he could get to the floor whenever he wanted, which was simply to put the British Encyclopaedia (tenth edition) on the top of his open shelves. He just pulled out a couple of volumes and held on, and down he came. And we agreed there must be iron staples along the skirting, so that he could cling to those whenever he wanted to get about the room on the lower level.

As we got on with the thing I found myself almost keenly interested. It was I who called in the housekeeper and broke matters to her, and it was I chiefly who fixed up the inverted bed. In fact, I spent two whole days at his flat. I am a handy, interfering sort of man with a screwdriver, and I made all sorts of ingenious adaptations for him – ran a wire to bring his bells within reach, turned all his electric lights up instead of down, and so on. The whole affair was extremely curious and interesting to me, and it was delightful to think of Pyecraft like some great, fat blow-fly, crawling about on his ceiling and clambering round the lintel of his doors from one room to another, and never, never, never coming to the club any more . . .

Then, you know, my fatal ingenuity got the better of me. I was sitting by his fire drinking his whisky, and he was up in his favourite corner by the cornice, tacking a

Turkey carpet to the ceiling, when the idea struck me. 'By jove, Pyecraft!' I said, 'all this is totally un-necessary.'

And before I could calculate the complete conse-quences of my notion I blurted it out. 'Lead under-clothing,' said I, and the mischief was done.

Pyecraft received the thing almost in tears. 'To be right ways up again—' he said.

I gave him the whole secret before I saw where it would take me. 'Buy sheet lead,' I said, 'stamp it into discs. Sew 'em all over your underclothes until you have enough. Have lead-soled boots, carry a bag of solid lead, and the thing is done! Instead of being a prisoner here you may go abroad again, Pyecraft! you may travel–'

A still happier idea came to me. 'You need never fear a shipwreck. All you need do is just slip off some or all of your clothes, take the necessary amount of luggage in your hand, and float up in the air–'

In his emotion he dropped the tack-hammer within an ace of my head. 'By jove!' he said, 'I shall be able to come back to the club again.'

The thing pulled me up short. 'By jove!' I said, faintly. 'Yes. Of course – you will.'

He did. He does. There he sits behind me now stuf-fing – as I live! – a third go of buttered teacake. And no one in the whole world knows – except his house-keeper and me – that he weighs practically nothing; that he is a mere boring mass of assimilatory matters, mere clouds in clothing, niente, nefas, and most in-considerable of men. There he sits watching until I have done this writing. Then, if he can, he will waylay me. He will come billowing up to me . . .

He will tell me over again all about it, how it feels, how it doesn't feel, how he sometimes hopes it is passing off a little. And always somewhere in that fat, abundant discourse he will say, 'The secret's keeping, eh? If anyone knew of it — I should be so ashamed . . . Makes a fellow look such a fool, you know. Crawling about on a ceiling and all that . . .'

And now to elude Pyecraft, occupying, as he does, an admirable strategic position between me and the door.

The Story of Prometheus

Time was when there were no gods. Then Uranus and Gaia – Heaven and Earth – joined together to give birth to the Titans, the gods who reigned before Zeus and the other deities of Olympus. Six of these Titans were so monstrous – three with fifty heads and a hundred hands, and three Cyclops, giants with one head and but a single eye – that Uranus banished them to eternal darkness in the underworld of Tartarus.

But Cronos, Uranus's youngest son, seized power from his father, made himself ruler of heaven and married another Titan called Rhea. Both Gaia and Uranus cursed Cronos for this, saying that one day he would be overthrown by one of his own children. This curse was a constant torment to Cronos's peace of mind, so that every time Rhea bore him a child he swallowed it whole, lest the curse might be fulfilled. When five of her children had been disposed of in this way, Rhea decided that that was enough. Before her sixth child was due to be born she hid herself in a cave and when the time came she handed her new-born babe, Zeus, to the mountain nymphs to be nursed. Then she found a large, smooth stone, wrapped it in swaddling clothes and brought it, saying it was her latest son, to Cronos, who, of course, immediately swallowed it.

When the infant god Zeus had grown big and strong under the tender care of the nymphs, he was told by one of them, Metis, that the time had come for him to avenge the wrongs committed by his father. So he introduced himself to Cronos's palace as a stranger and one day, when Cronos was drinking heavily, Zeus slipped a potent herb into his father's wine cup. This had the effect of making him vomit up all the five children he had swallowed – Poseidon, Hades, Hera, Demeter and Hestia. Now fully grown, two of them helped Zeus to bind their father in chains. But Cronos cried out for help to his Titan brothers and thus the war began between them and the younger gods. A few of the children of the Titans fought on the side of the young gods, prominent among them being Prometheus – wisest of all the Titans and gifted with special foresight. Thus he knew that Zeus was destined to overthrow the cruel Cronos and to begin the reign of the Olympians. Fighting alongside him was Epimetheus, who, however, unlike his great brother, possessed only hindsight.

It was Prometheus who interpreted for Zeus the Earth Mother's words telling him how he was to seek help against the Titans. Mother Earth sent Zeus to Tartarus to enlist the help of the Titan monsters imprisoned by Uranus in the everlasting darkness of the deepest regions under the earth.

The gates of Tartarus were guarded by a dreaded dragon, Campe, a fifty-headed she-monster. Her legs were writhing serpents and round her arms curled hissing snakes. Her body was scaly like a sea monster's and her tail had a scorpion's sting. Zeus slew this hideous beast with that same sword of adamant that Cronos had wielded to maim Uranus.

Now Zeus and the three sons of Uranus with fifty heads and a hundred hands sought out their Cyclops brothers and set them free. And the Cyclops forged weapons for the mighty war against the tyrant Cronos and the other Titans. For Poseidon they made a trident with which to lash the ocean to raging storm. For Hades they forged a helmet which made him invisible and for Zeus they created the crashing thunderbolt and the blinding, flashing lightning, mightiest of all weapons.

The heavens reeled, the earth trembled, the seas roared, as the battle raged with an almighty fury between the two armies.

And now from high Olympus Zeus hurled his thunderbolts and blinded the Titans with his lightning. The fifty-headed monsters threw rocks from each of their hundred hands, sending the Titans hurtling down to Tartarus, to the bottom-most regions of the underworld.

Thus Zeus became the ruler of the gods and he dwelt in Olympus. Hades gained the dark Erebus as his kingdom and Poseidon became the ruler of the seas.

Atlas, the most gigantic of all the Titans who fought

on the side of Cronos and who alone was not hurled down to Tartarus, was condemned by Zeus to bear the weight of heaven on his head and hands. But to Prometheus and Epimetheus, the Titans who had helped his cause, Zeus assigned responsibility for the world of man and animal.

Epimetheus began well. He gave great strength to the lion and tiger and all the fierce beasts of the forests. To birds he gave the gift of flight, and the seas and rivers to the fish, and the earth to the insects and all four-footed creatures.

Then Prometheus created man from the clay of the earth, watered with his own tears, for he loved the creatures he had made. With godlike compassion he did not endow them with a knowledge of the future, lest they should worry about the troubles that lay ahead. Instead he later gave them the great boon and blessing of Hope, so that they might always cherish some confidence that things would turn out for the best. He also created them in such a way that they would look upwards to heaven, not downwards to the earth like the animals of Epimetheus. He moulded men in the likeness of the gods themselves; he made them beautiful, he made them upright. And he taught them all that they needed to know, for they were naked and helpless.

Feeling that Zeus desired to have dominion over man, Prometheus tried a stratagem which might prevent this. At a meeting of gods and men to decide which portion of sacrifice was owed to the gods, Prometheus laid out an enormous ox which he had cut in a special way. He arranged the most succulent morsels in a skin and placed them on one side. On the other side he placed the bones covered in *a rich layer of fat*. Zeus, of course, had first choice and he naturally chose the fat-looking portion. Imagine his fury when he discovered nothing but bones underneath the fat. As a punishment he withheld fire from men and retained it as the exclusive preserve of the gods.

But the all-wise Prometheus knew where the forges were guarded. So he went to the island of Lemnos and stole a brand of fire which he enclosed in the hollow stalk of a fennel, and carried the flickering flame back to man. With this precious spark he kindled the first fire on earth. And he taught men how to use fire in the making of metals and tools and in all the arts and crafts, and in the cooking of their meats and the warming of their homes. Prometheus knew that he would have to pay dearly for this trickery, yet he was prepared to sacrifice himself, for without fire man would be little more than a beast.

Prometheus had defied the gods in the defence of man. Zeus sent Hephaestus, the smith god, to bind Prometheus with great chains to a rock on the topmost peak of the Caucasus on the eastern edge of the world. As if this punishment were not enough, an eagle was sent daily to pluck out his liver, which grew whole again each night, so that the rapacious bird could for ever renew its tormenting feast.

Zeus, fearful of what men might achieve with the gift of fire, schemed further to weaken their position. He caused the smith god, Hephaestus (who was likewise the inventor of all the crafts – lame and deformed though he was), to fashion a woman out of earth; she, by her charm, would bring misery and tragedy upon the race of mankind. And Zeus ordered the gods to bestow their gifts upon her according to their attributes and skills. She was moulded in the likeness of a goddess. Aphrodite, goddess of love, adorned her with dazzling beauty but filled her heart with painful yearning. Hermes, god of eloquence, gave her the power of speech but tainted her words with guile and cunning. She was called Pandora, which means 'the gifts of all'.

Then Zeus sent her as a companion to Epimetheus – the guileless Epimetheus, capable only of afterthought, when it was too late to think. He paid no heed to the warning of his far-seeing brother, Prometheus, that he must not accept gifts from Zeus. Then Hermes brought another gift from Zeus – a jar which had been filled by the gods – and Epimetheus was instructed that it must never be opened. As long as the lid remained on it, he was assured that man would enjoy a good life. So Epimetheus told Pandora to keep the jar in safety and warned her never to open it. From then on Pandora could think of nothing but the closed jar. What could it contain? She longed to take just one peep. And the day came when she could resist no longer. She raised the lid ... and out flew every conceivable evil thing, every trouble, nuisance and disease that has plagued mankind ever since. Fortunately for man, however, Prometheus had already placed his gift of Hope in the jar and that also flew out, thus giving him a blessing that would always soften his sufferings.

Meanwhile Prometheus continued to endure his torment on Mount Caucasus. His screams of agony sent earth-shattering echoes along the cliffs and amid the mountain chasms. Many a ship's crew fled in terror. Jason and the heroes of the Golden Fleece, as they sailed to Colchis on board the *Argos*, trembled with fear and pity as they saw the sinister eagle swoop to his feast of living flesh and the seas dyed red with the blood of Prometheus.

And Zeus sat on Olympus engulfed by an ever-growing terror of what the Fates might hold in store for him. For had it not been prophesied that Zeus himself would be overthrown, as he himself had overthrown his father before him? But how, and by whose hand, he was to fall, only the far-seeing Prometheus could tell, and Zeus knew too that Prometheus held the secret of how this could be avoided.

So Zeus sent his messenger, Hermes, to distant Caucasus with an offer to free the Titan from his torture if he would yield up his secret and tell Zeus how he might escape his doom. But Prometheus defied Zeus and all his threats of worse torment to come if he refused to speak.

'No menace from Zeus,' said Prometheus to Hermes,

'will force me to speak against my will. I can be freed if, and only if, Zeus from his heart bids me go free. If he will torture me more, then I shall endure what I have to endure. Yet in the end I *shall* be freed.' And Hermes cried, 'Then hear, O Prometheus, what great Zeus has decreed. Your torment shall continue and in the end you will be cast down into Tartarus for ever, and never shall you dwell amongst the immortals unless one other immortal can be found to take your place among the dead.'

Now Prometheus had also prophesied that a brood of giants would make war on the Olympians and as each giant would be struck down he would leap up again as strong as ever. No immortal could kill them, but a son of Zeus would be born a mortal man – greatest of all the heroes – and he alone would win for the gods the battle against the giants.

And so it was that Heracles, son of Zeus, slew the giants, as Prometheus had foretold.

Yet for many hundreds of years Prometheus hung in his chains on the mountain at the eastern edge of the world. But during this time Zeus had grown in wisdom. He had learnt that to rule by naked power and tyranny is not the right way. The great Titan's nobility in the face of suffering had softened his heart and he was moved to pity. He made the decision to release Prometheus and to ask for nothing in return. It came about like this. On his journey to the Hesperides to win the Golden Apples, the great Heracles was instructed by Zeus to ask Prometheus for his advice and help. Heracles's journey was long and arduous but at last he came to the mountain peak where Prometheus was chained. He saw the dread eagle swoop to its monstrous feast, he heard the agonized screams of the mighty Titan. Then, filled with rage and pity, Heracles drew his bow and let fly his deadly arrow. The voracious bird plummeted to the seas below. Heracles released the prisoner from his chains and Prometheus told him how to win the Golden Apples from the Garden of the Hesperides. Then Heracles told Prometheus to seek out the kind centaur Cheiron in the cave on Mount Pelion, for he had been wounded with a poisoned arrow aimed by Heracles himself at another centaur. Neither mortal nor immortal could heal his wound and now (continued Heracles) he prays for death, which, alas, cannot come, for he is immortal.

Forthwith Prometheus sought out Cheiron, who agreed to end his own sufferings when his tasks on earth were done and to take Prometheus's place in Erebus; and the great Heracles continued his journey, humbled by the grandeur and nobility of the mighty Titan.

Prometheus now came to Zeus and spoke: 'Neither bribes nor threats could make me speak, but now that you have put aside cruelty, I will reveal to you that which you had wished to know before and which has hitherto been kept secret. It has been foretold that the son of Thetis the sea-nymph will be greater than his father. Therefore do not wed Thetis, lest her son be your son.'

Zeus paid heed to these words and married Thetis to the hero Peleus. Their son was Achilles. When the wise Cheiron, great teacher of all the heroes of Greece, had taught Achilles all that heroes must know, he knew his work was accomplished, and so he passed on to Erebus to dwell amongst the dead.

Prometheus lived once again with the immortals, passing freely from Olympus to the earth as the helper of mankind.

DAMON RUNYON

A Piece of Pie

On Bolyston Street, in the City of Boston, Mass., there is a joint where you can get as nice a broiled lobster as anybody ever slaps a lip over, and who is in there one evening partaking of this tidbit but a character by the name of Horse Thief and me.

This Horse Thief is called Horsey for short, and he is not called by his name because he ever steals a horse but because it is the consensus of public opinion from coast to coast that he may steal one if the opportunity presents.

Personally, I consider Horsey a very fine character, because any time he is holding anything he is willing to share his good fortune with one and all, and at this time in Boston he is holding plenty. It is the time we make the race meeting at Suffolk Down, and Horsey gets to going very good indeed, and in fact he is now a character of means, and is my host against the broiled lobster.

Well, at the table next to us are four or five characters who all seem to be well-dressed, and stout-set, and red-faced, and prosperous-looking, and who all speak with the true Boston accent, which consists of many ah's and very few r's. Characters such as these are familiar to anybody who is ever in Boston very much, and they are bound to be politicians, retired cops, or contractors, because Boston is really quite infested with characters of this nature.

I am paying no attention to them, because they are drinking local ale, and talking loud, and long ago I learn that when a Boston character is engaged in aleing himself up, it is a good idea to let him alone, because the best you can get out of him is maybe a boff on the beezer. But Horsey is in there on the old Ear-ie, and very much interested in their conversation, and finally I listen myself just to hear what is attracting his attention, when one of the characters speaks as follows:

'Well,' he says, 'I am willing to bet ten thousand dollars that he can outeat anybody in the United States any time.'

Now at this Horsey gets right up and steps over to the table and bows and smiles in a friendly way on one and all, and says:

'Gentlemen,' he says, 'pardon the intrusion, and excuse me for billing in, but,' he says, 'do I understand you are speaking of a great eater who resides in your fair city?'

Well, these Boston characters all gaze at Horsey in such a hostile manner that I am expecting any one of them to get up and request him to let them miss him, but he keeps on bowing and smiling, and they can see that he is a gentleman, and finally one of them says:

'Yes,' he says, 'we are speaking of a character by the name of Joel Duffle. He is without doubt the greatest eater alive. He just wins a unique wager. He bets a character from Bangor, Me., that he can eat a whole window display of oysters in this very restaurant, and he not only eats all the oysters but he then wishes to wager that he can also eat the shells, but,' he says, 'it seems that the character from Bangor, Me., unfortunately taps out on the first proposition and has nothing with which to bet on the second.'

'Very interesting,' Horsey says. 'Very interesting, if true, but,' he says, 'unless my ears deceive me, I hear one of you state that he is willing to wager ten thousand dollars on this eater of yours against anybody in the United States.'

'Your ears are perfect,' another of the Boston characters says. 'I state it, although,' he says, 'I admit it is a sort of figure of speech. But I state it all right,' he says, 'and never let it be said that a Conway ever pigs it on a betting proposition.'

'Well,' Horsey says, 'I do not have a tenner on me at the moment, but,' he says, 'I have here a thousand dollars to put up as a forfeit that I can produce a character who will outeat your party for ten thousand, and as much more as you care to put up.'

And with this Horsey outs with a bundle of coarse notes and tosses it on the table, and right away one of the Boston characters, whose name turns out to be Carroll, slaps his hand on the money and says:

'Bet.'

Well, now this is prompt action to be sure, and if there is one thing I admire more than anything else, it is action, and I can see that these are characters of true sporting instincts and I commence wondering where I can raise a few dibs to take a piece of Horsey's proposition, because of course I know that he has nobody in mind to do the eating for his side but Nicely-Nicely-Jones.

And knowing Nicely-Nicely-Jones, I am prepared to wager all the money I can possibly raise that he can outeat anything that walks on two legs. In fact, I will take a chance on Nicely-Nicely against anything on four legs, except maybe an elephant, and at that he may give the elephant a photo-finish.

I do not say that Nicely-Nicely is the greatest eater in all history, but what I do say is he belongs up there as a contender. In fact, Professor D, who is a professor in a college out West before he turns to playing the horses for a livelihood, and who makes a study of history in his time, says he will not be surprised but what Nicely-Nicely figures one-two.

Professor D says we must always remember that Nicely-Nicely eats under the handicaps of modern civilization, which require that an eater use a knife and fork, or anyway a knife, while in the old days eating with the hands was a popular custom and much faster. Professor D says he has no doubt that under the old rules Nicely-Nicely will hang up a record that will endure through the ages, but of course maybe Professor D overlays Nicely-Nicely somewhat.

Well, now that the match is agreed upon, naturally Horsey and the Boston characters begin discussing where it is to take place, and one of the Boston characters suggests a neutral ground, such as New London, Conn., or Providence, R.I., but Horsey holds out for New York, and it seems that Boston characters are always ready to visit New York, so he does not meet with any great opposition on this point.

They all agree on a date four weeks later so as to give the principals plenty of time to get ready, although Horsey and I know that this is really unnecessary as far as Nicely-Nicely is concerned, because one thing about him is he is always in condition to eat.

This Nicely-Nicely-Jones is a character who is maybe five feet eight inches tall, and about five feet nine inches wide, and when he is in good shape he will weigh upward of two hundred and eighty-three pounds. He is a horse player by trade, and eating is really just a hobby, but he is undoubtedly a wonderful eater even when he is not hungry.

Well, as soon as Horsey and I return to New York, we hasten to Mindy's restaurant on Broadway and relate the bet Horsey makes in Boston, and right away so many citizens, including Mindy himself, wish to take a piece of the proposition that it is over-subscribed by a large sum in no time.

Then Mindy remarks that he does not see Nicely-

Nicely-Jones for a month of Sundays, and then everybody present remembers that they do not see Nicely-Nicely around lately, either, and this leads to a discussion of where Nicely-Nicely can be, although up to this moment if nobody sees Nicely-Nicely but once in the next ten years it will be considered sufficient.

Well, Willie the Worrier, who is a bookmaker by trade, is among those present, and he remembers the last time he looks for Nicely-Nicely hoping to collect a marker for some years' standing, Nicely-Nicely is living at the Rest Hotel on West Forty-ninth Street, and nothing will do Horsey but I must go with him over to the Rest to make inquiry for Nicely-Nicely, and there we learn that he leaves a forwarding address away up on Morningside Heights in care of somebody by the name of Slocum.

So Horsey calls a short, and away we go to this address, which turns out to be a five-storey walk-up apartment, and a card downstairs shows that Slocum lives on the top floor. It takes Horsey and me ten minutes to walk up the five flights as we are by no means accustomed to exercise of this nature, and when we finally reach a door marked Slocum, we are plumb tuckered out and have to sit down on the top step and rest a while.

Then I ring the bell at this door marked Slocum, and who appears but a tall young Judy with black hair who is without doubt beautiful, but who is so skinny we have to look twice to see her, and when I ask if she can give me any information about a party named Nicely-

Nicely-Jones, she says to me like this:

'I guess you mean Quentin,' she says. 'Yes,' she says, 'Quentin is here. Come in, gentlemen.'

So we step into an apartment, and as we do so a thin, sickly-looking character gets up out of a chair by the window, and in a weak voice says good evening. It is a good evening, at that, so Horsey and I say good evening right back at him, very polite, and then we stand there waiting for Nicely-Nicely to appear, when the beautiful skinny young Judy says:

'Well,' she says, 'this is Mr Quentin Jones.'

Then Horsey and I take another swivel at the thin character, and we can see that it is nobody but Nicely-Nicely, at that, but the way he changes since we last observe him is practically shocking to us both, because he is undoubtedly all shrunk up. In fact, he looks as if he is about half what he is in his prime, and his face is pale and thin, and his eyes are away back in his head, and while we both shake hands with him it is some time before either of us is able to speak. Then Horsey finally says:

'Nicely,' he says, 'can we have a few words with you in private on a very important proposition?'

Well, at this, and before Nicely-Nicely can answer aye, yes or no, the beautiful skinny young Judy goes out of the room and slams a door behind her, and Nicely-Nicely says:

'My fiancée, Miss Hilda Slocum,' he says. 'She is a wonderful character. We are to be married as soon as I lose twenty pounds more. It will take a couple of weeks longer,' he says.

'My goodness gracious, Nicely,' Horsey says. 'What do you mean lose twenty pounds more? You are practically emaciated now. Are you just out of a sick bed, or what?'

'Why,' Nicely-Nicely says, 'certainly I am not out of a sick bed. I am never healthier in my life, I am on a diet. I lose eighty-three pounds in two months, and am now down to two hundred. I feel great,' he says. 'It is all because of my fiancée, Miss Hilda Slocum. She rescued me from gluttony and obesity, or anyway,' Nicely-Nicely says, 'that is what Miss Hilda Slocum calls it. My, I feel good. I love Miss Hilda Slocum very much,' Nicely-Nicely says. 'It is a case of love at first sight on both sides the day we meet in the subway. I am wedged in one of the turnstile gates, and she kindly pushes on me from behind until I wiggle through. I can see she has a kind heart, so I date her up for a movie that night and propose to her while the newsreel is on. But,' Nicely-Nicely says, 'Hilda tells me at once that she will never marry a fat slob. She says I must put myself in her hands and she will reduce me by scientific methods and then she will become my everloving wife, but not before.'

'So,' Nicely-Nicely says, 'I come to live here with Miss Hilda Slocum and her mother, so she can supervise my diet. Her mother is thinner than Hilda. And I surely feel great,' Nicely-Nicely says. 'Look,' he says.

And with this, he pulls out the waistband of his pants, and shows enough spare space to hide War Admiral in, but the effort seems to be a strain on him, and he has to sit down in his chair again.

'My goodness gracious,' Horsey says. 'What do you eat, Nicely?'

'Well,' Nicely-Nicely says, 'I eat anything that does not contain starch, but,' he says, 'of course everything worth eating contains starch, so I really do not eat much of anything whatever. My fiancée, Miss Hilda Slocum, arranges my diet. She is an expert dietician and runs a widely known department in a diet magazine by the name of *Let's Keep House*.'

Then Horsey tells Nicely-Nicely of how he is matched to eat against this Joel Duffle, of Boston, for a nice side bet, and how he has a forfeit of a thousand dollars already posted for appearance, and how many of Nicely-Nicely's admirers along Broadway are looking to win themselves out of all their troubles by betting on him, and at first Nicely-Nicely listens with great interest, and his eyes are shining like six bits, but then he becomes very sad, and says:

'It is no use, gentlemen,' he says. 'My fiancée, Miss Hilda Slocum, will never hear of me going off my diet even for a little while. Only yesterday I try to talk her into letting me have a little pumpernickel instead of toasted whole wheat bread, and she says if I even think of such a thing again, she will break our engagement. Horsey,' he says, 'do you ever eat toasted whole wheat bread for a month hand running? Toasted?' he says.

'No,' Horsey says. 'What I eat is nice, white French bread, and corn muffins, and hot biscuits with gravy on them.'

'Stop,' Nicely-Nicely says. 'You are eating yourself into an early grave, and, furthermore,' he says, 'you are breaking my heart. But,' he says, 'the more I think of my following depending on me in this emergency, the sadder it makes me feel to think I am unable to oblige them. However,' he says, 'let us call Miss Hilda Slocum in on an outside chance and see what her reactions to your proposition are.'

So we call Miss Hilda Slocum in, and Horsey explains our predicament in putting so much faith in Nicely-Nicely only to find him dieting, and Miss Hilda Slocum's reactions are to order Horsey and me out of the joint with instructions never to darken her door again, and when we are a block away we can still hear her voice speaking very firmly to Nicely-Nicely.

Well, personally, I figure this ends the matter, for I can see that Miss Hilda Slocum is a most determined character, indeed, and the chances are it does end it, at that, if Horsey does not happen to get a wonderful break.

He is at Belmont Park one afternoon, and he has a real good thing in a jump race, and when a brisk young character in a hard straw hat and eyeglasses comes along and asks him what he likes, Horsey mentions this good thing, figuring he will move himself in for a few dibs if the good thing connects.

Well, it connects all right, and the brisk young character is very grateful to Horsey for his information, and is giving him plenty of much-obliges, and nothing else, and Horsey is about to mention that they do not accept much-obliges at his hotel, when the brisk young character mentions that he is nobody but Mr McBurgle and that he is the editor of the *Let's Keep House* magazine, and for Horsey to drop in and see him any time he is around his way.

Naturally, Horsey remembers what Nicely-Nicely says about Miss Hilda Slocum working for this *Let's Keep House* magazine, and he relates the story of the eating contest to Mr McBurgle and asks him if he will kindly use his influence with Miss Hilda Slocum to get her to release Nicely-Nicely from his diet long enough for the contest. Then Horsey gives Mr McBurgle a tip on another winner, and Mr McBurgle must use plenty of influence on Miss Hilda Slocum at once, as the next day she calls Horsey up at his hotel before he is out of bed, and speaks to him as follows:

'Of course,' Miss Hilda Slocum says, 'I will never change my attitude about Quentin, but,' she says, 'I can appreciate that he feels very bad about you gentlemen relying on him and having to disappoint you. He feels that he lets you down, which is by no means true, but it weighs upon his mind. It is interfering with his diet.

'Now,' Miss Hilda Slocum says, 'I do not approve of your contest, because,' she says, 'it is placing a premium on gluttony, but I have a friend by the name of Miss Violette Shumberger who may answer your purpose. She is my dearest friend from childhood, but it is only because I love her dearly that this friendship endures. She is extremely fond of eating,' Miss Hilda Slocum says. 'In spite of my pleadings, and my warning, and my own example, she persists in food. It is disgusting to me but I finally learn that it is no use arguing with her.

'She remains my dearest friend,' Miss Hilda Slocum says, 'though she continues her practice of eating, and I am informed that she is phenomenal in this respect. In fact,' she says, 'Nicely-Nicely tells me to say to you that if Miss Violette Shumberger can perform the eating exploits I relate to him from hearsay she is a lily. Goodbye,' Miss Hilda Slocum says. 'You cannot have Nicely-Nicely.'

Well, nobody cares much about this idea of a stand-in for Nicely-Nicely in such a situation, and especially a Judy that no one ever hears of before, and many citizens are in favour of pulling out of the contest altogether. But Horsey has his thousand-dollar forfeit to think of, and as no one can suggest anyone else, he finally arranges a personal meet with the Judy suggested by Miss Hilda Slocum.

He comes into Mindy's one evening with a female character who is so fat it is necessary to push three tables together to give her room for her lap, and it seems that this character is Miss Violette Shumberger. She weighs maybe two hundred and fifty pounds, but she is by no means an old Judy, and by no means bad-looking. She has a face the size of a town clock and enough chins for a fire escape, but she has a nice smile and pretty teeth, and a laugh that is so hearty it knocks the whipped cream off an order of strawberry shortcake on a table fifty feet away and arouses the indignation of a customer by the name of Goldstein who is about to consume same.

Well, Horsey's idea in bringing her into Mindy's is to get some kind of line on her eating form, and she is clocked by many experts when she starts putting on the hot meat, and it is agreed by one and all that she is by no means a selling-plater. In fact, by the time she gets through, even Mindy admits she has plenty of class, and the upshot of it all is Miss Violette Shumberger is chosen to eat against Joel Duffle.

Maybe you hear something of this great eating contest that comes off in New York one night in the early summer of 1937. Of course eating contests are by no means anything new, and in fact they are quite an old-fashioned pastime in some sections of this country, such as the South and East, but this is the first big public contest of the kind in years, and it creates no little comment along Broadway.

In fact, there is some mention of it in the blats, and it is not a frivolous proposition in any respect, and more dough is wagered on it than any other eating contest in history, with Joel Duffle a 6 to 5 favourite over Miss Violette Shumberger all the way through.

This Joel Duffle comes to New York several days before the contest with the character by the name of Conway, and requests a meet with Miss Violette Shumberger to agree on the final details and who shows up with Miss Violette Shumberger as her coach and adviser but Nicely-Nicely Jones. He is even thinner and more peaked-looking than when Horsey and I see him last, but he says he feels great, and that he is within six pounds of his marriage to Miss Hilda Slocum.

Well, it seems that his presence is really due to Miss Hilda Slocum herself, because she says that after getting her dearest friend Miss Violette Shumberger into this jackpot, it is only fair to do all she can to help her win it, and the only way she can think of is to let Nicely-Nicely give Violette the benefit of his experience and advice.

But afterwards we learn that what really happens is that this editor, Mr McBurgle, gets greatly interested in the contest, and when he discovers that in spite of his influence, Miss Hilda Slocum declines to permit Nicely-Nicely to personally compete, but puts in a pinch eater, he is quite indignant and insists on her letting Nicely-Nicely school Violette.

Furthermore we afterward learn that when Nicely-Nicely returns to the apartments on Morningside Heights after giving Violette a lesson, Miss Hilda Slocum always smells his breath to see if he indulges in any food during his absence.

Well, this Joel Duffle is a tall character with stooped shoulders, and a sad expression, and he does not look as if he can eat his way out of a tea shoppe, but as soon as he commences to discuss the details of the contest, anybody can see that he knows what time it is in situations such as this. In fact, Nicely-Nicely says he can tell at once from the way Joel Duffle talks that he is a dangerous opponent, and he says while Miss Violette Shumberger impresses him as an improving eater, he is only sorry she does not have more seasoning.

This Joel Duffle suggests that the contest consist of twelve courses of strictly American food, each side to be allowed to pick six dishes, doing the picking in rotation, and specifying the weight and quantity of the course selected to any amount the contestant making the pick desires, and each course is to be divided for eating exactly in half, and after Miss Violette Shumberger and Nicely-Nicely whisper together a while, they say the terms are quite satisfactory.

Then Horsey tosses a coin for the first pick, and Joel Duffle says heads, and it is heads, and he chooses, as the first course, two quarts of ripe olives, twelve bunches of celery, and four pounds of shelled nuts, all this to be split fifty-fifty between them. Miss Violette Shumberger names twelve dozen cherry-stone clams as the second course, and Joel Duffle says two gallons of Philadelphia pepper-pot soup as the third.

Well, Miss Violette Shumberger and Nicely-Nicely whisper together again, and Violette put in two five-pound striped bass, the heads and tails not to count in the eating, and Joel Duffle names a twenty-two pound roast turkey. Each vegetable is rated as one course, and Miss Violette Shumberger asks for twelve pounds of mashed potatoes with brown gravy. Joel Duffle says two dozen ears of corn on the cob, and Violette replies with two quarts of lima beans. Joel Duffle calls for twelve bunches of asparagus cooked in butter, and Violette mentions ten pounds of stewed new peas.

This gets them down to the salad, and it is Joel Duffle's play, so he says six pounds of mixed green salad with vinegar and oil dressing, and now Miss Violette Shumberger has the final selection, which is the dessert. She says it is a pumpkin pie, two feet across, and not less than three inches deep.

It is agreed that they must eat with knife, fork or spoon, but speed is not to count, and there is to be no time limit, except they cannot pause more than two consecutive minutes at any stage, except in case of hiccoughs. They can drink anything, and as much as they please, but liquids are not to count in the scoring. The decision is to be strictly on the amount of food consumed, and the judges are to take account of anything left on the plates after a course, but not of loose chewings on bosom or vest up to an ounce. The losing side is to pay for the food, and in case of a tie they are to eat it off immediately on ham and eggs only.

Well, the scene of this contest is the second-floor dining-room of Mindy's restaurant, which is closed to the general public for the occasion, and only parties immediately concerned in the contest are admitted. The contestants are seated on either side of a big table in the centre of the room, and each contestant has three waiters.

No talking and no rooting from the spectators is permitted, but of course in any eating contest the principals may speak to each other if they wish, though smart eaters never wish to do this, as talking only wastes energy, and about all they ever say to each other is please pass the mustard.

About fifty characters from Boston are present to witness the contest, and the same number of citizens of New York are admitted, and among them is this editor, Mr McBurgle, and he is around asking Horsey if he thinks Miss Violette Shumberger is as good a thing as the jumper at the race track.

Nicely-Nicely arrives on the scene quite early, and his appearance is really most distressing to his old friends and admirers, as by this time he is shy so much weight that he is a pitiful scene, to be sure, but he tells Horsey and me that he thinks Miss Violette Shumberger has a good chance.

'Of course,' he says, 'she is green. She does not know how to pace herself in competition. But,' he says, 'she has a wonderful style. I love to watch her eat. She likes the same things I do in the days when I am eating. She is a wonderful character, too. Do you ever notice her smile?' Nicely-Nicely says.

'But,' he says, 'she is the dearest friend of my fiancée, Miss Hilda Slocum, so let us not speak of this. I try to get Hilda to come and see the contest, but she says it is repulsive. Well, anyway,' Nicely-Nicely says, 'I manage to borrow a few dibs, and am wagering on Miss Violette Shumberger. By the way,' he says, 'if you happen to think of her, notice her smile.'

Well, Nicely-Nicely takes a chair about ten feet behind Miss Violette Shumberger, which is as close as the judges will allow him, and he is warned by them that no coaching from the corners will be permitted, but of course Nicely-Nicely knows this rule as well as they do, and furthermore by this time his exertions seem to have left him without any more energy.

There are three judges, and they are all from neutral territory. One of these judges is a party from Baltimore, Md., by the name of Packard, who runs a restaurant, and another is a party from Providence, R.I., by the name of Croppers, who is a sausage manufacturer. The third judge is an old Judy by the name of Mrs Rhubarb, who comes from Philadelphia, and once keeps an actors' boarding-house, and is considered an excellent judge of eaters.

Well, Mindy is the official starter, and at 8.30 p.m. sharp, when there is still much betting among the spectators, he outs with his watch, and says like this:

'Are you ready, Boston? Are you ready, New York?'

Miss Violette Shumberger and Joel Duffle both nod their heads, and Mindy says commence, and the contest is on, with Joel Duffle getting the jump at once on the celery and olives and nuts.

A Piece of Pie

It is apparent that this Joel Duffle is one of these rough-and-tumble eaters that you can hear quite a distance off, especially on clams and soups. He is also an eyebrow eater, an eater whose eyebrows go up as high as the part in his hair as he eats, and this type of eater is undoubtedly very efficient.

In fact, the way Joel Duffle goes through the groceries down to the turkey causes the Broadway spectators some uneasiness, and they are whispering to each other that they only wish the old Nicely-Nicely is in there. But personally, I like the way Miss Violette Shumberger eats without undue excitement, and with great zest. She cannot keep close to Joel Duffle in the matter of speed in the early stages of the contest, as she seems to enjoy chewing her food, but I observe that as it goes along she pulls up on him, and I figure this is not because she is stepping up her pace, but because he is slowing down.

When the turkey finally comes on, and is split in two halves right down the middle, Miss Violette Shumberger looks greatly disappointed, and she speaks for the first time as follows:

'Why,' she says, 'where is the stuffing?'

Well, it seems that nobody mentions any stuffing for the turkey to the chef, so he does not make any stuffing, and Miss Violette Shumberger's disappointment is so plain to be seen that the confidence of the Boston characters is somewhat shaken. They can see that a Judy who can pack away as much fodder as Miss

Violette Shumberger has to date, and then beef for stuffing, is really quite an eater.

In fact, Joel Duffle looks quite startled when he observes Miss Violette Shumberger's disappointment, and he gazes at her with great respect as she disposes of her share of the turkey, and the mashed potatoes, and one thing and another in such a manner that she moves up on the pumpkin pie on dead even terms with him. In fact, there is little to choose between them at this point, although the judge from Baltimore is calling the attention of the other judges to a turkey leg that he claims Miss Violette Shumberger does not clean as neatly as Joel Duffle does his, but the other judges dismiss this as a technicality.

Then the waiters bring on the pumpkin pie, and it is without doubt quite a large pie, and in fact it is about the size of a manhole cover, and I can see Joel Duffle is observing the pie with a strange expression on his face, although to tell the truth I do not care for the expression on Miss Violette Shumberger's face either.

Well, the pie is cut in two dead centre, and one half is placed before Miss Violette Shumberger and the other half before Joel Duffle, and he does not take more than two bites before I see him loosen his waistband and take a big swig of water, and thinks I to myself, he is now down to a slow walk, and the pie will decide the whole heat, and I am only wishing I am able to wager a little more dough on Miss Violette Shumberger. But about this moment, and before she as much as touches her pie, all of a sudden Violette turns her head and motions to Nicely-Nicely to approach her, and, as he approaches, she whispers in his ear.

Now at this, the Boston character by the name of Conway jumps up and claims a foul and several other Boston characters join him in this claim, and so does Joel Duffle, although afterward even the Boston characters admit that Joel Duffle is no gentleman to make such a claim against a lady.

Well, there is some confusion over this, and the judges hold a conference, and they rule that there is certainly no foul in the actual eating that they can see, because Miss Violette Shumberger does not touch her pie so far.

But they say that whether it is a foul otherwise all depends on whether Miss Violette Shumberger is requesting advice on the contest from Nicely-Nicely and the judge from Providence, R.I., wishes to know if Nicely-Nicely will kindly relate what passes between him and Violette so they may make a decision.

'Why,' Nicely-Nicely says, 'all she asks me is can I get her another piece of pie when she finishes the one in front of her.'

Now at this, Joel Duffle throws down his knife, and pushes back his plate with all but two bites of his pie left on it, and says to the Boston characters like this:

'Gentlemen,' he says, 'I am licked. I cannot eat another mouthful. You must admit I put up a game battle, but,' he says, 'it is useless for me to go on against this Judy who is asking for more pie before she even starts on what is before her. I am almost dying as it is, and I do not wish to destroy myself in a hopeless effort. Gentlemen,' he says, 'she is not human.'

Well, of course this amounts to throwing in the old napkin and Nicely-Nicely stands up on his chair, and says:

'Three cheers for Miss Violette Shumberger!'

Then Nicely-Nicely gives the first cheer in person, but the effort overtaxes his strength, and he falls off the chair in a faint just as Joel Duffle collapses under the table, and the doctors at the Clinic Hospital are greatly baffled to receive, from the same address at the same time, one patient who is suffering from undernourishment, and another patient who is unconscious from over-eating.

Well, in the meantime, after the excitement subsides, and wagers are settled, we take Miss Violette Shumberger to the main floor in Mindy's for a midnight snack, and when she speaks of her wonderful triumph, she is disposed to give much credit to Nicely-Nicely-Jones.

'You see,' Violette says, 'what I really whisper to him is that I am a goner. I whisper to him that I cannot possibly take one bite of the pie if my life depends on it, and if he has any bets down to try and hedge them off as quickly as possible.

'I fear,' she says, 'that Nicely-Nicely will be greatly disappointed in my showing, but I have a confession to make to him when he gets out of the hospital. I forgot about the contest,' Violette says, 'and eat my regular dinner of pig's knuckles and sauerkraut an hour before the contest starts and,' she says, 'I have no doubt this tends to affect my form somewhat. So,' she says. 'I owe everything to Nicely-Nicely's quick thinking.'

It is several weeks after the great eating contest that I run into Miss Hilda Slocum on Broadway and it seems to me that she looks much better nourished than the last time I see her, and when I mention this she says:

'Yes,' she says, 'I cease dieting. I learn my lesson,' she says. 'I learn that male characters do not appreciate anybody who tries to ward off surplus tissue. What male characters wish is substance. Why,' she says, 'only a week ago my editor, Mr McBurgle, tells me he will love to take me dancing if only I get something on me for him to take hold of. I am very fond of dancing,' she says.

'But,' I say, 'what of Nicely-Nicely Jones? I do not see him around lately.'

'Why,' Miss Hilda Slocum says, 'do you not hear what this cad does? Why, as soon as he is strong enough to leave the hospital, he elopes with my dearest friend, Miss Violette Shumberger, leaving me a note saying something about two souls with but a single thought. They are down in Florida running a barbecue stand, and,' she says, 'the chances are, eating like seven mules.'

'Miss Slocum,' I says, 'can I interest you in a portion of Mindy's chicken fricassee?'

'With dumplings?' Miss Hilda Slocum says. 'Yes,' she says, 'you can. Afterwards I have a date to go dancing with Mr McBurgle. I am crazy about dancing,' she says.

Acknowledgements

The editors are grateful for permission to use the following copyright material:

The Estate of P. G. Wodehouse for part one of 'The Mixer' by P. G. Wodehouse;

Rosemary Sutcliff for her story 'The Fugitives';

The National Trust for 'How Mowgli Entered the Wolf Pack' from *The Jungle Book* by Rudyard Kipling;

George G. Harrap & Company Ltd for 'Spit Nolan' from *The Goalkeeper's Revenge* by Bill Naughton;

Collins Publishers for 'Daedalus and Icarus' by Penelope Farmer;

The Society of Authors and the literary representatives of the Estate of John Masefield and Macmillan Publishing Co. Inc. for 'A Sailor's Yarn' from *A Mainsail Haul* by John Masefield, copyright 1913 by John Masefield, renewed 1941 by John Masefield;

Hamish Hamilton Ltd for 'Nine Needles' by James Thurber;

Penguin Books Ltd for 'What the Neighbours Did' by Philippa Pearce from *What the Neighbours Did and Other Stories* (Longman Young Books, 1972) pp. 9–20. Copyright © Philippa Pearce, 1972. Reprinted by permission of Penguin Books Ltd;

Acknowledgements

Jonathan Cape Ltd for 'Harriet's Hairloom' from *A Small Pinch of Weather* by Joan Aiken;

The Estate of H. G. Wells for 'The Truth About Pyecraft' by H. G. Wells;

Constable Publishers for 'A Piece of Pie' from *Runyon on Broadway* by Damon Runyon.

We should also like to express our thanks for their willing and valuable help to Hazel Wilkinson, Senior Lecturer at Hertfordshire College of Higher Education; the staff of Golders Green Library; Mrs S. Stonebridge, former Principal Children's Librarian, the Royal Borough of Kensington and Chelsea; Joan Butler, former Senior Assistant County Librarian, Services to Young People, Hertfordshire; Grace Hallsworth, West Herts Divisional Schools Librarian; Mrs D. Aubrey, former Senior Children's Librarian, Wandsworth Libraries; Christine Pountney, Youth Librarian, Schools Library Services, Redbridge; and the staff of Westminster City Library.

To Phyllis Hunt of Faber and Faber we are deeply indebted for her unfailingly patient help and wise counsel.

Professor G. P. Wells has very kindly permitted us to make a couple of minor alterations to the text of 'The Truth About Pyecraft' by H. G. Wells and for this we are grateful.

Heard about the Puffin Club?

... it's a way of finding out more about Puffin books and
authors, of winning prizes (in competitions), sharing
jokes, a secret code, and perhaps seeing your name in
print! When you join you get a copy of our magazine,
Puffin Post, sent to you four times a year, a badge and a
membership book.
For details of subscription and an application form; send a
stamped addressed envelope to:

The Puffin Club Dept A
Penguin Books Limited
Bath Road
Harmondsworth
Middlesex UB7 ODA

and if you live in Australia, please write to:

The Australian Puffin Club
Penguin Books Australia Limited
P.O. Box 257
Ringwood
Victoria 3134